CRUYFF

MATT & TOM OLDFIELD

CLASSIC
FOOTBALL HEROES

CRUYFF

FROM THE PLAYGROUND
TO THE PITCH

DINO

First published in the UK in 2025 by Dino Books,
an imprint of Bonnier Books UK,
5th Floor, HYLO, 105 Bunhill Row,
London, EC1Y 8LZ
www.bonnierbooks.co.uk

X @UFHbooks
X @footieheroesbks
www.heroesfootball.com
www.bonnierbooks.co.uk

Paperback ISBN: 978 1 78946 897 7
E-book ISBN: 978 1 78946 914 1

MIX
Paper | Supporting
responsible forestry
FSC
www.fsc.org   FSC® C018072

The authorised representative in the EEA is Bonnier Books UK (Ireland) Limited.
Registered office address: Floor 3, Block 3, Miesian Plaza
50–58 Baggot Street Lower,
Dublin 2, D02 Y754, Ireland.
Email: compliance@bonnierbooks.ie

A CIP catalogue record for this book is available from the British Library

Typeset by Envy Design Ltd
Printed and bound in Great Britain by Clays Ltd, Elcograf S.p.A

For Noah, Nico, Arlo and Lila

CLASSIC
FOOTBALL HEROES

Matt Oldfield is a children's author focusing on the wonderful world of football. His other books include *Unbelievable Football* (winner of the 2020 Children's Sports Book of the Year) and the *Johnny Ball: Football Genius* series. In association with his writing, Matt also delivers writing workshops in schools.

Cover illustration by Dan Leydon.
To learn more about Dan, visit danleydon.com
To purchase his artwork visit etsy.com/shop/footynews
Or just follow him on X @danleydon

TABLE OF CONTENTS

ACKNOWLEDGEMENTS

First of all I'd like to thank everyone at Bonnier Books for supporting me and for running the ever-expanding UFH ship so smoothly. Writing stories for the next generation of football fans is both an honour and a pleasure. Thanks also to my agent, Nick Walters, for helping to keep my dream job going, year after year.

Next up, an extra big cheer for all the teachers, booksellers and librarians who have championed these books, and, of course, for the readers. The success of this series is truly down to you.

Okay, onto friends and family. I wouldn't be writing this series if it wasn't for my brother Tom. I owe him so much and I'm very grateful for his belief in me as an author. I'm also very grateful to the rest of my family, especially Mel, Noah, Nico, and of course Mum and Dad. To my parents, I owe my biggest passions: football and books. They're a real inspiration for everything I do.

CHAPTER 1

"THE CRUYFF TURN"

19 June 1974, World Cup, Westfalstadion, Dortmund, Germany

There was a sold-out crowd packed into the stadium, and most of those fans had come to see one man: Johan Cruyff, the Netherlands superstar.

When Johan walked onto the pitch with his teammates, there was no hint of nerves. Instead, he strolled with the confidence of a man who had won three Ballon D'Or awards and three European Cups.

Pressure? What pressure?

Johan had been counting the days until the 1974 World Cup. International success was one of the last missing pieces in his football career, and he knew the

Netherlands had a real chance of lifting the trophy this time.

He had missed the World Cup four years ago, and he was determined to make up for lost time. The Netherlands had already won their opening match against Uruguay, and now they were facing Sweden in their second group game.

'The Swedes are going to have two defenders following you everywhere, so keep making your runs and drag them out of position,' legendary Netherlands boss Rinus Michels reminded Johan as they stood together on the touchline.

Johan nodded. He and Coach Michels had a long history together, starting with Johan's early days in the Ajax first team. They shared so many of the same football ideas that Coach Michels' team-talks were often short. He knew that Johan would be his coach on the pitch.

The fans sang louder, especially the Netherlands sections of the crowd with their orange shirts and scarves. Johan grinned, while feeling the same jolt of pride and excitement.

'Let's go, boys!' he shouted, stepping forward for the kick-off.

As Coach Michels had predicted, Johan had two Swedish shadows as he tried to get into space for a pass. When the ball went out for a throw-in, he jogged over to teammates Johan Neeskens and Piet Keizer, signalling for them to make forward runs when the defenders were distracted.

The Netherlands won possession, and Johan drifted over to the left wing, as he liked to do. For once, only one Sweden defender went with him – right-back Jan Olsson. Johan's eyes lit up when a long pass arrowed towards him.

He took a step forward to control the ball with his right foot, and then instinct took over. He was one-on-one against Olsson, and Johan lived for moments like this one.

He faked to cross the ball into the box straightaway and sensed Olsson falling for the trick. It was understandable in a way; Johan had fired in early crosses twice already in the first half.

But this time, he had a different plan. As Olsson got

ready to block the cross, Johan dragged the ball back with the inside of his right foot, sending it slightly behind him. In one movement, he turned back in the opposite direction and sprinted into the box. See ya!

The crowd responded with oohs and aahs, then a small groan when the cross was scrambled away. But there was now even more of a buzz around the stadium whenever Johan got the ball. The fans inched towards the edge of their seats, and the Sweden defenders looked like they had seen a ghost.

Despite all the Netherlands' attacks, the match finished 0–0, but Johan's magical moment was all anyone wanted to talk about afterwards. No one had seen that move before. 'The Cruyff Turn', they all called it.

'Was that something he had practised? Where had he learned it?'

'What made him use that skill today? Had he been saving it for the World Cup?'

Johan grinned at all the questions. The answers were quite simple. He had never seen it and never practised it. It was all pure football genius.

'It just sort of happened!' he said, smiling and shrugging.

That just added to the mystery, and the reporters instantly had their hands in the air again with more questions.

Johan already had a long list of career highlights, but this moment was definitely a new addition. On that night in Germany, there was no way for him to know that 'The Cruyff Turn' would live on for years to come as a skill for all young footballers to master and a fitting tribute to Johan's lifelong love of football – a love that had been there since the start.

CHAPTER 2

DESTINY ON THE DOORSTEP

'Johan!' came the call from downstairs. Though his full name was Hendrik Johannes Cruyff, everyone called him Johan.

At that moment, little Johan was bouncing his football on the floor. It made a nice sound. His parents, Manus and Nel, didn't always agree about that, and nor did his older brother Henny, but Johan never let the ball out of his sight.

He rushed down the stairs and burst into the kitchen, almost crashing into his dad, who was holding a basket of fruit. Manus just managed to keep his balance.

'Whoa!' Manus called out. 'Careful, Johan! This nearly ended up on the floor!'

'Sorry, Dad!' Johan replied, picking up the ball before either of his parents noticed it.

He was just about to take the ball outside when his dad said something that made him freeze on the spot.

'I'm going over to the stadium to give the food to the injured Ajax players and then I'll be back,' Manus explained to Nel, while putting on his jacket.

Johan raced over and wrapped his arms around Manus's leg.

'Can I come?' Johan asked hopefully. 'Please! Please!'

'Well…' Manus started, looking over at Nel.

It wasn't the first time that Johan had asked that question, and they both knew it wouldn't be the last. Manus and Nel often sent baskets from their fruit and vegetables shop for players who were injured or ill, and Johan knew that was usually a chance to meet some of the Ajax team.

'It's dry outside so you could cycle over together,' Nel suggested, smiling when she saw Johan's eyes light up like it was Christmas morning.

Johan was still only five years old, but his love for

ver since he was a baby. Back

in a tiny outfit that matched

d it always seemed to put

. The Ajax stadium was just

up the ... Cruyffs' home, and Johan felt
like he could sense the action from their doorstep on
match days.

Manus was usually in the crowd for home games,
so Johan waited eagerly at the door and tried to guess
what was happening on the pitch before his dad
returned in the evening to give him his match report.
Today, though, Johan would be seeing everything at
Ajax for himself!

'I wonder who'll be there!' Johan said excitedly as
he joined his dad for the bike ride. 'I hope we can see
the pitch!'

By the time they got to the stadium, Johan could
feel his heart beating faster. Disappointingly, it was
mostly deserted – no players, no coaches. But that
didn't stop Manus from giving Johan a little tour.

Johan walked with his dad from the main building
towards the pitch, worrying for a tiny moment that

this was all a dream, and he would soon wake up in his bed at home.

'It's a nice day for a visit!' a voice called, snapping Johan out of his daydream.

He and Manus turned around. A man was standing on the pitch, holding some tools and waving to them.

'Hi, Henk!' Manus shouted. He turned to Johan. 'That's Henk. He's the club groundsman. He keeps this place looking good.'

Henk walked over and shook hands with Johan, who had a curious look on his face.

'What kinds of things do you do?' Johan asked.

'I water the grass and make sure it's ready for the next game,' Henk explained. 'Then I mark the white lines and the penalty spots. The last job is usually putting up the nets on the goalposts. It's a bit of everything, really. That's probably why I'm so tired by the end of the day!'

Johan was listening but also enjoying the thrill of being so close to where his Ajax heroes played.

Henk looked over and saw Johan's face.

'You know, I'm always saying how useful it would

be if I had a helper to get through some of the jobs,' he said. 'Maybe someone who lives close to the stadium and was available at weekends.'

It took Johan a minute to understand what Henk was saying. 'Wait, you mean... me?' he asked.

'We'd have to make sure your dad was okay with it, but yes, you seem like the perfect choice for the job!' Henk said.

Manus grinned. 'How can I possibly say no, now?!'

'But I have to tell you, Johan,' Henk continued. 'You might have to speak to the players sometimes. Do you think you could handle tha...?'

'Yes! Yes!' Johan interrupted.

Manus laughed. 'Well, I guess we'll be back next weekend then!' he said.

CHAPTER 3

"THE BOY WITH THE BALL" AND THE CONCRETE VILLAGE

'Johan, how many times have I told you about that ball?!' his teacher said suddenly.

Uh-oh. Johan looked up and realised that the teacher had stopped the lesson mid-sentence, distracted by the sound of Johan tapping his football from one foot to the other under his desk.

'Sorry!' he said, with a shy smile. He stared at the paper in front of him and held his breath, hoping this wouldn't be reported back to his parents.

Johan tried to focus while at school, but part of his

brain always seemed to have skipped ahead to break-time and lunchtime, when he could play football with his friends. Some of the other kids just called him 'The Boy with the Ball', because they didn't know anything else about him. He was always in too much of a hurry to stop and talk to them.

The teachers didn't have much sympathy when it was time to give progress reports to Johan's parents:

'He's got potential, but he needs to work harder.'

'Some afternoons, it's like he's in a daydream and forgets he's at school.'

'School can't compete with football for his attention.'

Sitting at the table for supper, Manus and Nel reminded Johan that he had to take his schoolwork seriously.

'We know you want to be a football player, but it's good to have a backup plan too,' Nel said gently. 'School can give you that.'

'Unfortunately, none of the tests are about Ajax players, though!' Henny teased.

Johan's football obsession didn't end when he was

at home, though. He had to get to what they called the 'Concrete Village' for his next game. Among all the small homes in the neighbourhood, there were some quiet streets with space to play football. If it was warm enough, the kids were all outside playing there, and Johan was always ready to test himself against other boys from the neighbourhood. This was his chance to unleash all his extra energy, and he came home each night sweaty and tired.

It was there that Johan met Wim, another football-mad boy who lived in the Concrete Village.

'Hey, I'm an Ajax fan too!' Johan said, spotting Wim's red-and-white scarf.

'One day, we're going to be champions of Europe!' Wim replied with a grin. 'We might be fifty years old by then, but it's going to happen!'

'Especially if they put you and me up front!' Johan added, high-fiving his new friend.

'I'm on Johan's team!' Wim called out, sprinting into position before anyone could argue.

Often, it started as 3 v 3, or 5 v 5. Then within minutes there were twenty kids racing up and down the street. Jumpers and jackets were thrown into a pile to make goalposts, and the games went on until it was too dark to see anymore.

The Concrete Village games were fast and furious, but they taught Johan a lot. On the busiest nights, there were kids everywhere, and he had to make sure his control was perfect to get away from tacklers. His feet had to be fast to dodge defenders and keep his balance – and there was always the risk of cuts and scrapes. It only took one tumble for Johan to end up with blood dripping down his knees.

He also had to get creative when he was trapped in tight spaces. One evening, he dribbled forward but two defenders cut him off before he could look up to play a pass. *Well, there's only one option left*, he thought. At the last second, Johan kicked the ball against the side of the pavement.

The other boys froze. What was Johan doing? There was nobody standing over there.

But Johan knew exactly what he was doing. Using the pavement for a one-two, he darted away to get to the rebound as the ball bounced back towards him. He took another touch and fired a shot past the goalkeeper.

Goooooooooooooooooooooooooaaaaaaaaaaaaaaaaaaaa aaaaaaalllllllllllllllllllllllllllll!

'Whoa, this boy's got all the moves!' Wim shouted, jumping on Johan's back.

Soon, all the other kids were trying to copy that move, but no one could do it as effortlessly as Johan.

'I've got to admit, little bro,' Henny said, after joining one of the games. 'You play like you're the King of the Village.'

Nothing made Johan happier than playing in these games. Well – almost nothing. There was one other place that always put a smile on his face.

CHAPTER 4

"NEED ANOTHER PLAYER?"

The Ajax stadium had become Johan's second home. Henk always had jobs for him, and it gave him a rush of excitement every time he saw the dressing rooms and the pitch.

Soon everyone knew Johan's name, and he was treated like a member of the club. Dribbling his ball wherever he went, he was in his football paradise.

Manus had told him lots of stories about the Ajax players, and every extra detail made them even bigger heroes for Johan. He was usually lost for words when he saw them.

'Ger van Mourik and Wim Bleijenberg walked into the room and I didn't know what to say!' he told

Henny. 'It was like I'd lost my voice and could only make little mumbling sounds!'

Henny laughed. 'Don't worry, you'll get other chances,' he said. 'I'm sure they didn't even notice.'

Johan always had his backpack with him for the bike ride to the stadium, but not because he needed to bring clothes or tools for his work with Henk… It was because he was hoping to play!

Johan had heard stories about training sessions where Ajax were short of players and needed any willing volunteers to join in. Sometimes it was the kit man or one of the coaches or even Henk. From that day onward, Johan always brought his football boots – just in case.

'You never know,' Johan told his parents. 'One of these days, I might be in the right place at the right time!'

When Johan arrived on a wet Wednesday evening, he knew there would be a few urgent jobs to protect the pitch from the rain. But the weather wasn't bad enough to stop the Ajax coaches working with the first-team players.

Johan immediately noticed that it seemed like a

smaller group that day – maybe injuries or illnesses had limited the numbers. He could hear the coaches shouting instructions as the players ran a lap of the pitch then split into pairs to work on passing drills.

For the last part of the session, the coaches put the players into two teams for a mini game. Johan crept closer, noticing again that there were fewer players than usual.

Before he could stop himself, he opened his mouth. 'Do you need another player?' he called.

The coaches turned around, looking confused at first. Then one of them recognised Johan as the tiny, skinny figure who scampered around with Henk.

The coaches looked at each other and smiled. They knew what this moment would mean for Johan, who would tell anyone who would listen about his love for Ajax.

'Actually, that would really help us out,' one of the coaches said. 'That team has one fewer player so you'll be with them.' He pointed to the far side of the little pitch.

Before the coach could change his mind, Johan

jumped in the air and ran over to get his boots. The Ajax players may have thought it was ridiculous to have a nine-year-old on the pitch with them, but none of them showed it. Instead, they encouraged Johan whenever he got the ball. The rain continued, but he didn't even notice.

He ran up and down and tried to keep up, but his little legs were no match for the Ajax players. On a few occasions, he realised he was just standing still in amazement watching the players' skill – how they controlled the ball, how they passed so accurately and how they kicked the ball so hard.

By the end, he was lying on the wet grass and breathing heavily.

'Great effort, Johan,' someone said, and a hand reached out to help him get back on his feet.

Johan looked up and almost fell back down again when he saw it was Ger, one of Ajax's best defenders.

'Thanks!' Johan said. 'Today was amazing!'

'You're a really good little player,' Ger replied, patting Johan on the back. 'Keep working hard and you could be training here regularly when you're older!'

Johan couldn't wait to share his stories. He cycled home through puddles, and burst into the house when he got back.

'Mum! Dad!' he yelled as he opened the front door.

Manus and Nel appeared with worried looks on their faces. 'What's happened?' Nel said, looking out into the rain and thinking about Johan on his bike. 'Are you hurt?'

'No, no, nothing like that,' he said. 'I was helping Henk and then the Ajax team needed another player, so I joined in with their training match!'

Johan couldn't stop smiling.

'Who was on your team?' Manus asked, also with a grin on his face. 'Who did you think the best players were?'

Suddenly his dad was asking questions with the same curiosity that Johan usually had when talking about Ajax.

'It's a day I'll never forget, that's for sure,' Johan said.

As he lay in bed that night, he replayed the game in his head. It was just one practice, but he felt a step closer to becoming a real footballer.

CHAPTER 5

THE YOUTH TEAM INVITE

All that time Johan spent around the club paid off when he heard about the Ajax youth team. But before he could rush to find out more about the team, the team found him instead.

One afternoon, Johan, Wim and the usual group of kids from the neighbourhood were in the middle of their latest game in the Concrete Village. Cheers, laughter and the occasional argument filled the air, but nothing could distract Johan from one of his best games.

Some of the boys followed the ball, kicking and running aimlessly. Johan was different, though. With his skinny body, he couldn't overpower defenders, but he made up for that with clever runs and bursts of speed.

That day, Johan had already scored two goals and set up two more for Wim. As he put his hands on his knees and tried to catch his breath, he spotted a man on the pavement who looked familiar. Had he seen him before?

That thought quickly vanished – for now. The game was back on, and Johan rushed to help his teammates.

Then, as the man moved a little closer, Johan realised who it was. Jany van der Veen, the Ajax youth coach. Johan had seen him a few times at the stadium with the other coaches.

'Hi, I'm Coach Jany,' he said, stepping forward and shaking Johan's hand. 'I was just going to watch for a few minutes, but then you started playing like a little wizard, so I had to stay!'

Johan smiled. 'You picked the right day!' he said.

Coach Jany laughed. 'Where did you learn to play like that?' he asked.

'Here!' Johan answered. 'We play every day. Plus, I'm around the Ajax training sessions a lot, so maybe some of that magic rubbed off on me!'

Coach Jany paused, like he was deciding whether

or not to say what he was thinking. 'You've probably heard that we're looking for players for the Ajax youth teams,' he said eventually. 'How old are you? Eight?'

'I'm ten,' Johan replied, trying to stand a little taller.

'Oh great!' Coach Jany said, taking a piece of paper out of his pocket. 'Here are the details for training, if you're interested.'

'Yes, yes, I'm interested!' Johan replied in a hurry. 'I'll tell my parents tonight. What's next? Is there a trial?'

'No, I don't think we'll need that,' Coach Jany said, with a smile. 'I saw enough today to know that you're ready for this. Welcome to the Ajax youth team!'

Johan felt like his heart might jump out of his chest. For a couple of seconds, he stood there, mouth open, trying to find the right words.

'Th…That's amazing!' he managed at last.

He skipped home, humming and grinning. He still couldn't really believe it.

This was just what Johan had been hoping for. The Concrete Village games were fun, but he was desperate to test himself in proper matches on proper pitches. That was the next step to really develop his skills, surrounded by talented teammates who shared the same football dreams.

'You're not going to believe this!' Johan said to his family as they sat down for dinner.

Manus laughed. 'Let me guess, is it about Ajax?'

'Am I that predictable?!' he replied. 'Yes, it is, but it's not about the first team. Well maybe one day... but not yet...'

'Slow down, Johan!' Nel said, smiling and putting an arm on his shoulder. 'What do you mean?'

'One of the Ajax coaches was watching our street game tonight, and he invited me to join the Ajax youth team!' Johan explained.

'Wow, Johan, that's incredible!' Manus said, bursting with pride that his son had been recruited by his favourite team. 'Do we need to take you for a trial?'

'That's what I asked!' Johan answered. 'But Coach Jany has already given me a spot.'

'It must have been quite a performance tonight!' Nel said.

'Just a few goals and a few assists,' Johan answered, pretending it was nothing.

As he was finishing his meal, he pictured similar goals and assists – but this time wearing an Ajax shirt.

'Maybe we'll be in the crowd to watch you one of these days!' Nel added, wrapping Johan in a big hug.

CHAPTER 6

FAMILY HEARTBREAK

But then, suddenly, Johan's world was turned upside down. He would always remember where he was standing when he got the terrible news: that his dad had died that afternoon from a heart attack.

In that moment, Johan was supposed to be celebrating his school graduation with his friends. But he had no interest in that anymore. With tears rolling down his cheeks, he and Henny rushed home to be with their mum.

It was so sudden. One moment Manus was there, the next he was gone. Johan just couldn't understand it. He kept thinking his dad would walk in through the door.

As the family tried to make sense of it all, they had lots of questions to answer. Would they keep the shop open? How would they afford to pay the rent?

'I don't know, sweetheart,' Nel said, when Johan asked whether they would have to move and find a new home.

Friends and neighbours helped whenever they could, but the Cruyff family had no choice but to try to move on with their lives. Every day was painful, but they found a way to be brave.

'We have to get back into a routine,' Nel said. 'That will help.'

School and football. School and football. School and football. That had always been Johan's routine, and he focused on that even more now. He didn't know any other way to cope.

But some changes were unavoidable, whether they liked it or not.

'It's time to close the shop,' Nel said one evening in a sad voice. 'I know that's not easy to hear, but I just can't keep it going on my own.'

Johan and Henny nodded. They understood how

difficult all of this was for their mum, and they did their best to make life simpler for her whenever they could.

But just as the Cruyffs were starting to really worry about the future, Ajax came to the rescue. The club had heard about their struggles and remembered their kindness over the years, from fruit baskets to vegetable deliveries.

'You're part of our family,' the Ajax management told Nel. 'Don't panic. We'll speak to a few of our contacts and I'm sure we can sort out some work for you.'

'Thank you so much,' Nel replied. 'This means the world to me. I'll take any job you can find.'

The next day, there was already an answer. Ajax had arranged a cleaning job for Nel, working for one of the Ajax coaches, as well as some extra hours cleaning the dressing rooms at the stadium.

That was a huge relief. Other people helped too. Henk had been a regular guest for meals over the years and he was even more important for the family now. He kept an eye on Johan at the stadium, and all the coaches were so kind, checking on Johan to make sure he was eating and sleeping.

Now, Johan needed football more than ever. On the pitch, he could shut out all his other thoughts and focus on the game. He arrived early for practices, and sometimes stayed so late that the Ajax staff had to come and find him before locking up the building.

'Just five more minutes,' he often pleaded. 'Please!'

The coaches sometimes wished that Johan would slow down and give his body a chance to recover, but there was no doubt that he was improving at a rapid pace. Soon, he was a few steps ahead of the other boys in his age group – and even the age groups above.

'You were right, Jany!' one of the other coaches said after the latest training session. 'Johan isn't the fastest or the biggest or the strongest, but that boy is a football genius.'

'He'll keep getting better too,' Jany replied. 'He sees the game unlike any youngster I've ever coached, and we've got him on our team.'

Alone, with a ball at his feet, Johan allowed himself to dream again. He was so determined to succeed at

Ajax – and do it for his dad, who had always been such a big supporter.

'Don't worry, Dad,' Johan said quietly to himself one night before going to bed. 'Ajax's future is in good hands.'

CHAPTER 7

NEW TARGETS WITH COACH JANY

During Johan's progress through the Ajax youth system, he was introduced to new teammates and new football ideas.

'Training is meant to be fun, boys,' Coach Jany said, standing in the centre circle with his youth team players sitting around him. 'Sure, it's about hard work too, but we'll try to disguise that with drills that really make you think.'

Johan always looked forward to seeing what Coach Jany had planned for each session. The same core skills were at the heart of every practice – passing, dribbling, shooting, heading and ball control – but he found different ways to work on them.

'If you can master these skills, football is a simple game,' Coach Jany said. 'That's the secret for everything we do on the pitch.'

There was still lots of running, with laps of the pitch and sprints across the penalty area, but the number one objective was being comfortable on the ball.

Johan was quiet in training. He knew some of the other local boys from their Concrete Village battles, but sometimes he felt shy or just preferred to dribble around on his own before the sessions started.

'What position do you play?' Coach Jany asked one of the boys.

'Striker,' came the reply.

'By the end of this season, you might have a different answer,' Coach Jany explained. 'You'll try different positions on the pitch and use your skills in different ways. Just because you played as a striker or midfielder or defender in the past, that doesn't mean you can't learn other positions.'

Johan understood Coach Jany's point. They were all footballers, and the top players could do it all. At this age, it was too early to really know what anyone's best position was.

One evening, Coach Jany put the players into pairs for two-on-two battles. One pair would attack, and the other pair would defend.

'This is a chance to work on a few of our core skills,' he said. 'For one pair, it's all about defending and tackling. For the other, it's a mix of dribbling and passing. You've got to get past the defenders and stop the ball next to the cone.'

These were the drills that Johan loved, and no one wanted to be against him. He was paired with a boy called Gerrie, who jogged over with a big grin on his face.

'At least I won't have to defend against you this week!' Gerrie said.

Against the first few pairs, Johan put on a show, weaving between tackles and sprinting to the cone.

Gerrie jogged over for a high-five. 'I'm here if you need me,' he said.

Johan looked over and realised this drill probably wasn't as much fun for Gerrie if he didn't ever get the ball.

'Okay, time for a new plan,' Johan whispered. 'I'll start with the ball again, but as soon as the other boys focus on me, make a run towards the cone and I'll pass it through to you.'

Gerrie grinned and nodded.

Sure enough, their opponents expected another Johan solo run. One boy was marking him while the other was hovering near enough to rush over and help. Johan gave Gerrie a quick look to say 'Now!', and then he took one more touch to tempt both defenders towards the ball.

At the last second, he poked a pass between them into the open space behind, and Gerrie raced clear. He even had time for a pretend yawn before stopping the ball by the cone.

That was the first of many drills where Johan and Gerrie teamed up, starting a new friendship.

'Are you going to Bram's party on Friday?' Gerrie asked after one training session. They both knew Bram, a local boy, who had invited a group of friends over to his house.

Johan shook his head. 'Not this time,' he replied.

'We've got a big game on Saturday, so I need to focus on that.'

'Your brain doesn't have room for anything that's not football, does it?' Gerrie joked.

In a way, that was true, though. Most of the other boys picked up their bags and went home as soon as practice was over. But Johan always wanted more time. He usually guzzled more water then jogged back over to the pitch. It didn't matter if no one else stayed with him. He was perfectly happy doing some extra work on his own.

He would kick the ball high into the air and control it on his foot. Then he would flick it up onto his chest, then down to his thigh.

Next, he would take two of the balls over to the nearest net and fire shot after shot after shot until his leg ached.

He kept remembering what Ger van Mourik had told him at practice a few years ago: keep working hard. He was taking that advice seriously. No one was going to work harder than Johan.

CHAPTER 8

BRUISING HITS AND DIRTY KITS

'Your kit is on your bed!' Nel called as Johan and Wim got back from another game at the Concrete Village. 'We'll need to wash it on Saturday night so it's ready for the matches on Sunday.'

'How many teams do you play for?!' Wim asked, looking at Johan like he was an alien.

Johan laughed. Sometimes it felt like the answer was ten. Ajax were testing him at different age groups within the youth system. That meant being ready to play on Saturday and Sunday – and even twice in the same day.

He hurried up the stairs and saw the beautiful red-and-white Ajax shirt, white shorts, and red-and-white socks.

It was hard to believe that the kit had been covered in mud last weekend.

Johan could still picture the moment. He had sprinted to reach a pass and dribbled into the box when a defender tripped him from behind, sending Johan flying into a puddle of wet mud.

Yesssss! A penalty!

But nooooo! His shirt and shorts were caked in mud.

He was still angry about the foul when he got home. His mum opened the door and froze at the sight of Johan, who was still wearing his kit and even had mud on his nose and forehead.

After a long pause, Nel burst out laughing.

'Is that the new brown Ajax kit?' she teased.

It wasn't quite as funny later that night, when Nel tried to get the muddy stains out of the kit, scrubbing and rinsing over and over again.

Johan was doing the same thing outside with a bucket of soapy water and his muddy boots. This was all part of the deal. It wasn't as if there was a team of people standing by at Ajax to do it, and Johan always felt proud when his boots were clean again.

A few weeks later, Johan limped into the kitchen and sat down at the table. Even just that simple movement was painful. This time, it was a defender's knee that had done the damage. Instead of mud on his kit, it was a purple bruise on his thigh.

'I think I upset one defender too many,' Johan said, grinning. 'But it'll take more than that to stop me!'

'I know there's probably no such thing for you as too much football,' Nel said. 'But are you sure this is good for your body? You're still only a teenager.'

'I'm fine, I promise,' Johan replied. 'Football is my happy place, and this is the best way for me to keep improving.'

In fact, he was so desperate to be on the pitch that he even helped out as a goalkeeper for one of the Ajax teams. At least he wasn't likely to get injured there.

All of this experience had one goal in mind: promotion to the first team. That was Johan's dream, and it was a regular discussion topic for the Ajax coaches. It was a difficult decision. If they pushed Johan forward too soon, it could be too overwhelming for him. If they waited too long, Johan might get frustrated.

'We can't hold him back any longer,' Coach Jany said during one meeting. 'He's too good. He dribbled past five defenders in the youth team practice today, and he was the best player on the pitch yesterday with the reserve team.'

'It's a great example for the other young kids too,' another coach added. 'It gives them something to aim for. It shows them that our youth teams can lead them to the first team.'

There were nods around the table. 'So, let's tell Johan,' said Coach Vic Buckingham, manager of the Ajax first team. 'I'm looking forward to working with him!'

Johan thought he might faint when he heard the news. He wasn't nervous – he believed he was good enough to play in the first team – but it still caught him by surprise to get the call-up so soon.

'Congratulations, Johan,' Coach Buckingham said. 'You've got a bright future ahead of you!'

Johan shook his hand and tried to sort through the

hundreds of questions in his head. 'When do I start?' he asked with a grin.

'How does next week sound?' Coach Buckingham replied.

'Perfect!' Johan answered. 'Absolutely perfect!'

After Johan took off his boots, he headed for the shower, punching the air in celebration. This was it!

His Ajax dream had reached the next level, and he felt ready for the challenge.

CHAPTER 9

DEBUT DELIGHT

By now, Johan had been around Ajax long enough to learn about Dutch football. Most of the players were only semi-professional. That meant they had other jobs to focus on when they weren't at Ajax. One was a butcher, another was a builder, and a third owned a newspaper shop. It was incredible to see how committed they were to football, while still juggling so many other responsibilities.

It wasn't like that everywhere, though. Johan had read about other leagues that were further ahead, where the players were full professionals.

'One day, Dutch football is going to catch up,' he told his friends. 'We have to get to that level.'

The first team was a big step up for Johan in a lot

of ways, especially with so many of his heroes in the squad with him. But it didn't change anything about the way he approached his football – and it didn't take long for him to shine as the brightest star in training.

Sure, Johan was only seventeen, but Coach Buckingham had made it clear: 'If you're good enough, you're old enough.'

After one dribbling run at practice past three first-team defenders, Coach Buckingham turned to another coach. 'Try telling our defenders that Johan isn't ready to start for this team!' he said, with a little grin.

The next day, Johan looked up to see Coach Buckingham signalling to him. The latest drill had finished, and the other players were taking a quick break. Johan jogged over, hoping it was good news.

'Ever you since you joined the first team squad, your attitude has been fantastic,' Coach Buckingham said. 'That counts for a lot with me. There were never any doubts about your talent, and I can see you work as hard as anyone. Even though we've been careful about rushing you into the team, you've earned your chance.'

He paused, leaving Johan guessing. So…? The suspense was unbearable.

'So…' Coach Buckingham continued. 'You'll be starting for us this weekend.'

Johan wasn't sure how to react. He wanted to jump and scream. He talked himself out of that, but there was no way he could respond coolly. A big smile spread across his face as he shook Coach Buckingham's hand. 'I can't wait!' he said. 'I won't let you down!'

Now Johan had to work out how he was going to sleep for the next few nights. His whole body was tingling with excitement, and he had a million different emotions. He told his mum, Henny, Henk and Wim, but then kept the news quiet after that – just in case Coach Buckingham changed his mind.

On the day of the game, Johan woke early and went into the kitchen. 'It's just another game,' he told himself.

Ajax lost 3–1 to GVAV that afternoon, but Johan made every second count. First-team regulars Piet Keizer and Bennie Muller did their best to relax him with jokes during the warm-up, and Johan felt an extra burst of energy in his legs when the referee got the game started.

The nerves disappeared after a few good touches, and soon he was calling for the ball. He darted away from his marker a couple of times and saw the GVAV defenders arguing about how to stop him.

Even with Ajax trailing 3–0, Johan kept making runs forward – and then at last, one of them paid off. He reached a loose ball first and finished past the keeper.

Goooooooooooooooooooooooaaaaaaaaaaaaaaaaaaa aaaaaaalllllllllllllllllllllllllllllll!

There weren't a lot of smiles in the dressing room after the loss, but all his teammates stopped by to congratulate Johan on his debut.

'That was the first of many Ajax goals, I'm sure!' Coach Buckingham said, patting Johan on the back. 'Well played!'

The good news continued when Johan signed a professional contract with Ajax that summer. He was earning real money now.

'I'll be looking out for the new car you've bought for me,' Wim joked when he saw Johan in the street.

Best of all, Johan's contract meant a fresh start for his family after some very difficult years.

'Mum, you're not cleaning the dressing room ever again!' Johan told her. 'We can relax now.'

Nel smiled. 'Your dad would be so proud of you!' she said.

Johan smiled too. 'I was just thinking the same thing,' he replied.

CHAPTER 10

TOTAL FOOTBALL

Johan could feel change in the air at Ajax from the morning that Coach Rinus Michels arrived, replacing Coach Buckingham. He remembered Coach Michels from his playing days – Rinus had been a striker at Ajax in Johan's early days helping Henk – and now he was curious to see what this new era would mean for the club.

From the very start, everything Coach Michels said pointed to a more professional club with full-time players, daily training and better facilities. During his first meeting with the players, he took out a big sheet of paper.

'Who's ready to shake up the football world?' Coach Michels asked.

Most of the players just stared back at their new boss. But Johan grinned. He liked the sound of that.

'Look, most teams have a winger on the right, a winger on the left, and at least one striker in the centre, here,' Coach Michels said, drawing three circles on his paper. 'And most teams keep those players in those positions. The right winger is meant to spend the whole game on the...'

'Right wing,' Johan answered.

'Exactly, and that makes life easier for defenders,' Coach Michels continued. 'They always know where the right winger or left winger or striker will be. But I want us to try something different, with flowing movement that makes defenders dizzy. It's going to change the game.'

Johan's brain was whirring now, picturing what this would look like in a real match, and he was soon firing more questions at Coach Michels.

'How much freedom will we have?' he asked. 'Would strikers and midfielders swap positions?'

'You'll be our striker, but you're free to go wherever you want, dragging defenders with you,'

Coach Michels replied. 'Our wingers can drift around the pitch too, our midfielders can fill the gaps, and our opponents are going to have a tough time marking everyone.'

This was the first of many football conversations that combined the creativity of Johan and Coach Michels.

'Teams are going to see us lined up in a normal formation and they'll have no idea what's coming!' Johan said, grinning at the thought.

'As long as we're all connected, we'll be a step ahead when we win the ball back too,' Coach Michels said.

Some of the players had doubts about this new approach, but Johan was a believer.

'Let's give it our best shot,' he told his teammates. 'If this works, we could be real contenders.'

'You would say that!' Piet teased. 'You and Coach are best mates.'

Johan smiled. 'Not always,' he shot back. 'Are you forgetting the cross-country run last week?!'

That made them all laugh. But Johan hadn't been

laughing at the time. Coach Michels had sent the squad on a long run through the woods, but Johan had decided on his own plan – and a different route. He had raced off to a fast start, then ducked behind some bushes until all the other players had rushed past. Once it was all quiet, he snuck out and found a shortcut to rejoin the group before the finish line.

'I was sweating and panting, and you just jogged past me with a wink,' Piet said, shaking his head.

'I just had to stop and catch my breath, that's all,' Johan said, laughing again. But Coach Michels had figured out his shortcut – and Johan had ended up with extra running.

On the pitch, the results with the new system soon won everyone over. Ajax began to dominate, and they were having fun too. Best of all, with Johan gliding around the pitch and creating chances, they couldn't stop scoring:

5–1 against ADO Den Haag,

7–0 against Utrecht,

5–1 against Groningen…

'That's Total Football!' Coach Michels said proudly

after Ajax's latest victory. 'That's the only way to describe it.'

'It's the start of something special,' Johan joined in. 'I can feel it!'

Ajax were top of the Dutch league heading into the last few weeks of the season, and they were so close to a famous turnaround after some disappointing years.

'Don't relax now!' Coach Michels yelled after a sloppy drill in training. 'We haven't won anything yet!'

Johan scored another hat-trick to bring Ajax a step closer, and they had one hand on the trophy. A few weeks later, the party could officially start.

'Champions!' Piet shouted. 'That sounds pretty good!'

'And we're hungry for more!' Johan added.

CHAPTER 11

THE NETHERLANDS' NEW HERO

Johan was still getting used to his shift from professional footballer to star player. Life felt different after winning the league. More people recognised him around the city and wanted a quick conversation or an autograph. He did his best to make time for all of them.

As the 1966–67 season kicked off, Johan was so focused on Ajax's upcoming games that he hadn't really thought about the international matches scheduled on the calendar. So he almost shrieked into the phone when the Netherlands manager Georg Kessler called to tell him he was in the squad for the team's Euro 1968 qualifier against Hungary. Nothing could really shake Johan's confidence, but playing for his country was a big deal.

He didn't know what to expect when he joined the rest of the Netherlands squad. He was the nineteen-year-old rising star that everyone was praising. How would the other players feel about that?

There was no time to worry, though. He just had to prove himself in training. Johan's football brain quickly understood how Coach Kessler wanted the team to play, and he knew he could fit well in that system.

Indeed, Johan made such a good first impression that he was thrown straight into the starting line-up to face Hungary.

'Remember to enjoy yourself tonight,' Coach Kessler told him. 'You only get to make your international debut once!'

'Make your runs and we'll play the passes to get you free,' added Sjaak, one of the team's midfielders. 'We know you only need a yard of space to work your magic.'

Johan quickly saw that none of the Hungary defenders knew how to handle his movement.

Every long ball created panic, and he was just waiting for the right pass to take advantage.

On the next attack, he cushioned a clever layoff, but he didn't just stop and admire the silky touch – he turned and sprinted behind the defence.

The through ball arrived right on time and now it was a sprint race. Johan got there first, and he kept the ball on his left foot, making it harder for the chasing defender to block his shot.

He charged into the penalty area and unleashed a rocket strike that almost ripped through the net.

Gooooooooooooooooooooooooaaaaaaaaaaaaaaaaaaaa aaaaaaalllllllllllllllllllllllllllll!

His teammates had their arms in the air in amazement. What a strike!

'It took me ages to score my first international goal,' one of his teammates shouted. 'It only took you fifty-four minutes!'

The Netherlands had to settle for a 2–2 draw, but Johan was the centre of attention yet again.

'You're making a habit of debut goals!' Henny said when he saw Johan at the weekend.

But his fast start to international football was soon
on hold after a red card in his next game for arguing
with the referee. While he walked off the pitch,
Johan kept staring at the floor. The frustration of
being fouled all game had bubbled up, and he had
lost control for a second. It was a silly mistake and
a painful lesson, because it meant an international
suspension. He would have to wait before he got to
wear the famous orange shirt again.

'You'll learn from it,' Wim said, trying to cheer him
up. 'There's nothing you can do about it now. Don't
worry – everyone still loves you!'

He was right. The red card didn't take anything
away from the Johan hype. He had made his mark,
and the Netherlands fans had a new hero to lead
the team forward. That's all anyone was interested in.

If anything, the international ban made Johan even
more determined to dominate with Ajax. Back with
his club teammates, he had a point to prove, and
that was bad news for the rest of the league.

He even set himself a new target of thirty goals.
With Piet and Klaas Nuninga alongside him, the

Ajax attack was unstoppable.

In the first game of the season, Johan sent a message to the rest of the league: good luck beating us! He scored a hat-trick that day in a 7–0 win, showing no mercy at all to the Elinkwijk defence.

'It's going to be a big year!' he said to himself as he arrived at the Ajax stadium for their next league game. 'Watch out, defenders!'

CHAPTER 12

THE FOG GAME

Even with the recent success in the Dutch league, Johan knew that Ajax would have to make progress in the European Cup before people outside the Netherlands took them more seriously. That was his goal heading into the 1967–68 season. But no one thought they had much of a chance when they had to play Liverpool in the second round.

'Give them respect but don't show them fear,' Coach Michels reminded his players. 'Liverpool are used to teams playing defensively against them, but we're going on the attack from the start.'

As Johan walked onto the pitch with his teammates, it wasn't the noise of the crowd that made him stop suddenly. It was the fog in the air all around the stadium.

'I've never seen anything like this!' said Ajax captain Frits Soetekouw. Johan heard his voice, but he could barely see him through the thick fog.

'Are we still going to play?' they all wondered.

But there was no official announcement, so Johan brushed it off. There could be no excuses tonight. This was Ajax's chance to send a message to the rest of Europe.

For the next ninety minutes, everything went to plan. Ajax scored an early goal, and they were soon on the attack again. It was hard enough to stop Johan on a regular day, but he was even more dangerous in the foggy conditions.

'Keep shooting!' Johan called to his teammates. 'Any shot has a chance of going in with this weather.'

Klaas followed Johan's advice, sweeping a quick shot towards the bottom corner on a counterattack. The Liverpool keeper scrambled to save the shot, but Johan was the fastest to react to the rebound, tapping the ball into the empty net.

Goooooooooooooooooooooooaaaaaaaaaaaaaaaaaaaa aaaaaaalllllllllllllllllllllllllllll!

'Don't ease off now!' Coach Michels shouted from the touchline. 'Keep pushing for another goal!'

Ajax were adjusting to the difficult conditions better than Liverpool – and in no time it was 4–0. The first leg finished 5–1, and the whole crowd rose to cheer Johan and his teammates at the final whistle.

But the tie wasn't over, and Anfield was rocking for the second leg. The Ajax players all looked a little more nervous when they returned to the dressing room.

'If the crowd is loud now, what's it going to be like at kick-off?!' Klaas said as he sat down next to Johan.

'They're going to throw everything at us!' Coach Michels told his players. 'Remember, they probably think we only won the first leg because of the fog. We've got to earn their respect all over again tonight.'

Coach Michels was still pacing around the changing room when the players got back at half-time with the score locked at 0–0. But there was no need for him to worry. Johan had brought his shooting boots.

When Piet escaped down the left wing, he whipped in a cross that bobbled through to Johan. Suddenly, he was one-on-one with the keeper from ten yards out. Johan knew exactly what he was going to do, tilting his body slightly to the left and opening up enough room to fire a right-footed shot high into the net.

Goooooooooooooooooooooooaaaaaaaaaaaaaaaaaaaa aaaaaaallllllllllllllllllllllllllllll!

With Liverpool pushing forward, Johan had even more space now, and he was on the move again as Ajax launched another quickfire move down the left wing. When a low cross skidded towards him, he was totally unmarked, and he slid to poke the ball into the bottom corner.

Goooooooooooooooooooooooaaaaaaaaaaaaaaaaaaaa aaaaaaallllllllllllllllllllllllllllll!

The game ended 2–2, but Ajax had made their statement. They had knocked out the mighty Liverpool, and Johan was in the middle of all the hugs as the subs and coaches rushed onto the pitch.

Ajax's European adventure ended in the next round, but the confidence from outplaying Liverpool carried them to the Dutch title for the second year in a row, finishing five points ahead of Feyenoord.

Some days, Johan felt like he couldn't miss. He had scored in every single one of his first 14 league games that season, on the way to 33 total league goals, and he was even on the scoresheet in the Dutch Cup final as Ajax clinched that trophy in extra-time.

As Johan packed his suitcase for a summer break, he had earned the attention of teams, scouts and fans across Europe. They were all buzzing about this young Ajax magician who was on the path to being an all-time great.

CHAPTER 13

DANNY

Johan was happy in his football bubble, getting up early
to practice and staying late for more skills and drills.
Eat, sleep, football. That had been his routine for years,
and it seemed to be working just fine.

But it could be lonely at times, especially if he was the
only one on the pitch, and he knew it was important to
find a balance. When he was invited to Piet's wedding,
he was hesitant, but lots of the other Ajax players were
going and he knew it would be rude not to go.

'You never know, you might meet someone there,'
Piet said, trying to persuade Johan to join them.

Johan laughed and rolled his eyes. Yeah, right,
he thought.

But his attitude soon changed at the wedding party when a pretty young woman sat down next to him at the table.

'You're Johan, right?' she asked. 'I'm Danny. Nice to meet you.'

As all the couples went up to the dance floor, Johan and Danny had the table to themselves.

'So, where do you work?' Danny asked.

'Oh, well… I'm… I'm a football player,' Johan said, caught by surprise. These days, it was unusual for anyone not to know who he was. 'I play for Ajax, with Piet… I'm Johan Cruyff… you might have…'

Danny burst into laughter, and Johan realised she was teasing him. She knew exactly who he was.

'I did pretty well,' she said. 'I was sure I was going to start laughing straight away. It's just a shame I fell apart before you explained even more about who you are!'

'Oh yeah, a real shame!' Johan shot back, grinning.

For once, he was happy not to be talking about football. Danny was kind and funny, and she told great stories. Maybe Piet was right after all!

Later in the evening, Johan turned to face Danny and saw her looking at him, with her head leaning to one side, then the other.

'Do I have something on my face?' he asked, reaching for a napkin.

Danny laughed. 'No, it's not that,' she explained. 'I was just thinking you'd look good with longer hair.'

Johan laughed. 'You're kidding, right?'

'No, really!' she insisted. 'People look up to you. You're Mr Ajax these days. Show them you've got style.'

'What if I don't have style?' Johan replied, grinning.

'Oh, I think you do!' she said, smiling back.

It had turned into a magical night for Johan, and he even had a chance to dance with Danny before the end of the party. That was the start of a whirlwind adventure, with more dates and trips. Soon, Johan felt like he had known her his whole life.

A year later, he and Danny were at another special party – their own wedding.

By now, Johan had met all of Danny's family, and he was working closely with her dad, Cor, who was joining him for his business conversations with

Ajax. With family and friends packed into a big hotel ballroom for the wedding, Johan and Danny looked forward to their next chapter together.

While Johan walked up to the microphone, his mum joined him and straightened his tie before hurrying back to her table. 'Sorry, old habits!' Nel said, giggling.

He kept his speech short and everyone stood and clapped. Every little detail of the party felt perfect, and the night flew by at lightning speed.

'Can you believe this yet?' Johan whispered, staring around the room then back at Danny in her white dress.

'That you managed to win me over?' she teased.

Johan grinned. 'No, can you believe that we're married?!' he said.

'It's everything I've ever wanted,' she replied, leaning over to kiss him on the cheek. 'Wherever we are, we'll be having fun as long as we're together.'

Johan felt the same way. They were a team, and Danny was the best teammate he could have wished for.

CHAPTER 14

HARD LESSONS LEARNED

'Are you ever going to let someone else win the league?' Danny asked, with a smile. Ajax had won three Dutch league championship titles in a row – in 1966, 1967, 1968.

Johan looked at her. 'The other teams can try,' he said. 'But no one has been good enough yet.'

Sometimes Johan wished that he could savour the big achievements for longer. Other players and coaches had probably been celebrating all summer, but his brain didn't work like that. It was always about the next challenge and the next competition.

He knew that Ajax had a target on their backs now, with their rivals desperate to stop them, and that meant fighting even harder to stay at the top.

But it was tough to keep up the high standards year after year. When Ajax's results slipped just a little in the 1968–69 season, it was enough for Feyenoord to swoop in. All year, Johan had felt confident that Ajax would find a way to close the gap, but at the end of the season he was sitting in a silent dressing room. Finishing second hurt.

'Keep your heads up,' Coach Michels said. 'The biggest game of our season is still ahead.'

Johan nodded. That was the right way to look at it. Ajax's results in Europe had improved, and they were in the 1969 European Cup Final, proving they belonged alongside the top teams from other countries.

It took some Johan magic to get there, with three goals in the quarter-final against Benfica and another in the semi-final against Spartak Trnava. But Total Football was alive and well, and the final at the Bernabéu Stadium in Madrid was a chance to go into the history books forever.

Johan didn't get nervous very often, but he could

feel his heart beating a little faster while putting on his boots before his first ever European Cup Final. He knew how hard it was to get this far in the tournament. This might be his only opportunity to win it.

'It's the biggest game of my life,' he had told his mum before leaving for Madrid. He meant it. It didn't get any bigger than facing the mighty AC Milan with the European Cup up for grabs.

All week, they had talked about getting an early goal. Instead, they conceded one. That nightmare of a start floored Ajax, and AC Milan took control of the game, cruising to a 4–1 win.

Johan sat down on the pitch while the AC Milan players celebrated behind him. He didn't want to get up. He didn't want to accept that the game was over. It felt like he had been punched in the stomach.

'We didn't play our best when it mattered most,' Johan said, back in the dressing room. He put his head in his hands and stayed like that as the disappointment fully sank in.

Johan heard all the efforts to cheer the players up.

'There's always next year.'

'We'll be an even stronger team next season after this experience.'

'This will be extra motivation for a great preseason.'

He believed all of those points. But it didn't make things better that night, and he didn't want to wait another year.

He couldn't stay in a bad mood for long, though, especially when Ajax kept winning trophies. Winning the league and cup double during the 1969–70 season put a smile back on his face, and he was going to need to find more space at home to keep all his medals.

As in previous summers, Johan enjoyed the break, but he couldn't wait to be back on the pitch. The start of the 1970–71 season was a little different, though. When he hobbled off with a leg injury, he feared the worst. The next day, it felt twice as bad.

The Ajax doctor examined his leg, and his first comment made Johan wince more than the injury itself. 'You'll need to rest it,' the doctor said.

All Johan could do was follow the doctor's instructions. He couldn't join in with training and he couldn't even kick a ball. While his leg was healing, though, he could at least start some recovery exercises.

'This feels like the worst punishment,' he told Danny. 'I just wish I was on the pitch with my teammates.'

'Even the very best players go through ups and downs,' she reminded him. 'I know it's tough, but you'll be back on the pitch soon, and then you're going to do more amazing things. I can feel it.'

CHAPTER 15

KINGS OF EUROPE

*2 June 1971, European Cup Final, Wembley
Stadium, London*

During the Ajax players' journey to England for
the 1971 European Cup Final, there was one main
thought on their minds: we can't waste this second
chance. This was their opportunity to get rid of the
bad memories from the 1969 final.

Johan was in a better mood these days. He had
bounced back from the injury, even changing his
shirt number to 14 to signal this new start, and
away from the game, he and Danny had welcomed
little Chantal into the world. But he could still

remember the horrible feeling of sitting on the pitch after the final whistle two years ago and could still feel the sting of coming so close to a historic achievement.

That loss to AC Milan had been one of his darkest days in the first team. He hadn't lost many big games, and he still thought about that match at least once a week.

'We've got some unfinished business with this trophy!' he said, while he and Piet walked into the hotel where the team were staying.

The journey back to the final had been tough, but now only Panathinaikos, a strong team from Greece, stood between Johan and the big prize.

Even though some of Johan's teammates had played in the previous European Cup Final, there were a lot of nervous faces around the room when Coach Michels gathered the squad for a meal. The pressure was on, and they all knew it.

'Forget about last time,' Coach Michels said, noticing the same tension at the table. 'This is a whole new game, and we're a better, stronger team now. Sometimes you just have to go through those difficult experiences to grow and learn.'

Johan nodded. It wasn't really the nerves that were bothering him. It was more the excitement and impatience for the game to begin. He would have happily put down his knife and fork and played the final right then. Instead, the minutes and hours ticked by slower than ever.

At last, it was game time, and Ajax made a dream start with an early goal. But there were still some anxious moments.

'Stay connected!' Coach Michels called. 'We need more movement!'

It wasn't the best Ajax performance. Not even close. But they kept battling. No one was willing to let this game slip away, and Johan was everywhere, tracking back one minute then sprinting forward on another attack.

In the final minutes, Johan surged down the right wing and tried to give the Ajax defenders a chance to catch their breath. Panathinaikos players backed off towards the penalty area, so he kept going, danced past one tired tackle and flicked a pass through to teammate Arie Haan.

Arie's shot was deflected but it looped over the goalkeeper and into the net. Game over!

Johan rushed over and joined the celebrations. 'Yeeessssssssss!!!'

The Ajax fans were singing, the coaches all looked ready to rush onto the pitch and Johan dropped to the floor when he heard the final whistle.

'We did it!' Johan shouted, jumping up and hugging Piet. 'We're the Kings of Europe!'

The long walk up the Wembley stairs was the last thing the Ajax players needed after an exhausting ninety minutes, but Johan knew it would be worth it when they got to the top. The European Cup would be waiting for them!

Ajax captain Velibor Vasović led the way, and Johan caught sight of the shimmering trophy just a few yards away. It looked even more spectacular, up close!

Velibor checked that all his teammates were ready to cheer, then lifted the trophy into the air. The party continued in the dressing room – and back at the hotel. Johan didn't want the night to end.

'These moments last forever,' Coach Michels reassured him. 'You'll always be a European champion.'

Johan was soon holding another trophy. He was invited for the Ballon D'Or award ceremony, recognising the year's best player, and he beamed proudly when his name was announced as the winner.

With Danny and little Chantal by his side, Johan walked up to the stage in his Puma blazer and received the award – a shiny golden ball on a little rectangular base. It felt surprisingly light in his hands.

The photographers took photos before Johan was even ready to smile, and the flashes blinded him for a few seconds.

'You're the first Dutch player and the first Ajax player to win the Ballon d'Or,' the presenter said, smiling. 'Congratulations on an incredible year!'

As Johan sat with the trophy, he thought about some of the highlights from that season. There were so many to choose from – and he and Ajax were just getting started.

CHAPTER 16

TWO IN A ROW FOR "TOTAL FOOTBALL"

31 May 1972, European Cup Final, De Kuip Stadium, Rotterdam

'If we want to become an all-time great team, we can't be satisfied with last year's success,' Johan told his teammates before the start of the 1971–72 season.

That message took some of the pressure off new manager Stefan Kovács, who was walking into a dressing room that was full of strong characters. With Coach Michels swapping Ajax for Barcelona, it was a new chapter at the club, but the story didn't change much. With Johan's goals and assists, they reclaimed the Dutch title, defended the Dutch Cup and made it back to the European Cup Final for a chance to prove they were still the number one team.

This night was the chance to complete a perfect year. They were facing Inter Milan in Rotterdam, which meant a short trip for the Ajax fans, and Johan heard them roaring as soon as he stepped out of the tunnel to warm up.

He took a deep breath and focused on the job ahead. They were one special performance away from becoming even bigger Ajax legends.

'Let's wear them out with our movement,' he told Piet and Gerrie. 'They'll be exhausted in the second half.'

Everyone knew Johan was the danger man. Sure enough, swarms of Inter defenders crowded round him every time he got the ball. Sometimes, he laid it off quickly, giving his teammates room to attack. But he was still confident enough to take them on, spinning, gliding, dribbling forward and looking for gaps.

'The goal is coming!' he yelled after one missed chance. 'Keep the energy up!'

Leading the way like he loved to do, Johan set off on a solo run at the start of the second half, and it took a desperate tackle to stop him. But that got the Ajax fans on their feet. Johan waved his arms, calling for them to cheer even louder.

Then he got the chance he was waiting for. The Inter goalkeeper jumped for a looping cross but collided with one of his defenders. Johan's eyes lit up as the ball bounced towards him. He took a touch to control it, steadied himself, then smashed a shot into the empty net. 1–0!

Gooooooooooooooooooooooooooaaaaaaaaaaaaaaaaaaaa aaaaaaalllllllllllllllllllllllllllll!

Johan leapt and punched the air, while his teammates huddled around him.

'There was no way you were missing that!' Arie said with a grin, and they all jogged back to the halfway line.

Ajax couldn't relax yet, though, and Johan knew it. Inter were still up for the battle. 'We need another goal,' he thought.

When Ajax won a corner, Johan drifted into the

box. He wasn't one of the biggest players, but he was always working on his heading, with some of the same drills that Coach Jany had taught him years ago.

This time, the ball dipped perfectly for him, and Johan powered a header past the keeper. 2–0!

Goooooooooooooooooooooooooaaaaaaaaaaaaaaaaaaaa aaaaaaalllllllllllllllllllllllllllllll!

'How did they leave you free like that?!' Piet said, mouth open in shock.

'Maybe they thought he wouldn't want to mess up that beautiful hair!' Gerrie joked.

Johan felt like he was floating, as the rest of his teammates rushed over to him. Two goals in the European Cup Final – that was the kind of thing he had dreamed about in his Concrete Village matches. What a feeling!

The referee blew the final whistle, and Johan was getting flashbacks to last season when the Ajax players crowded round him to celebrate European Cup glory again. He was limping a little from some of the rough tackles and he was sure he had bruises all over his shins. But he didn't mind. Well – not until his teammates all piled on top of him.

'Watch it!' Johan joked. 'Don't you think I've had enough people pushing and tripping me today?!'

With an easy journey home, many Ajax fans had stayed in the stadium, and Johan waved to the crowd while the players enjoyed their lap of honour. There were Ajax scarves and Netherlands flags everywhere, making it almost feel like a home game.

'We're still the team to beat!' Johan said, and meanwhile Piet raised the trophy high into the air.

Even for Johan, who had lifted a lot of trophies in the last few years, this was an incredible night. A second straight Ballon D'Or award was the icing on the cake, and Johan was still smiling as he, Danny and Chantal headed off for a summer of rest. More than ever, they needed it.

Most people now believed that Johan was the best footballer on the planet, and he was going to do his best to live up to that title.

CHAPTER 17

UNSTOPPABLE/
HAT-TRICK HEROES

'There was Pelé, and now there's Cruyff,' a TV presenter said. 'Those are the two greatest players ever.'

That was the level that Johan had reached. A few years ago, he would have laughed at comparisons with Pelé, but Ajax's recent success had brought more fans and more attention.

More accurately, it had brought more fans and more attention for Johan. He didn't really notice that difference at first, but it was there. When some people talked about Ajax, they made it sound like 'Johan and ten other guys'.

Sometimes he heard that in games too when

opponents were trying to get an angry reaction. 'Don't worry, Ajax are a one-man team!' came the shouts. 'If you stop Johan, you stop Ajax!'

But how could it be a problem? Ajax were sweeping aside everyone they played, and Johan didn't really think about it. He knew everyone was playing their part in the team's success, so why did it matter if the reporters mainly just wanted to speak to him?

'Winning two European Cups in a row is special,' Coach Kovács said during a meeting early in the season. 'But a hat-trick of European Cups would put us in a whole different category.'

'Is it true that we get to keep the trophy permanently if we win three in a row?' Arie asked.

'Yes, that's right,' Coach Kovács replied. 'That specific trophy will be ours, and they'll make a new one for the next season. But we've got to get there first!'

Johan accepted the challenge. Ajax quickly had the Dutch league under control, and their experience in big games led to a third straight European Cup Final, this time against Juventus.

'I'm just as excited as I was for my first final,'

Johan said, while he and Danny sat together outside.
'It's the match that everyone wants to play in, and the
best players find an extra level in the biggest games.'

'Just remember, you can't do it all on your own,'
she replied.

This final was extra special for Johan. As captain,
he would be leading the team onto the pitch and that
feeling gave him goosebumps. He loved the extra
responsibility.

'Ready to make history?' he asked his teammates
Johnny Rep and Johan Neeskens during the
countdown to kick-off.

After so many finals together, the Ajax players knew
that a fast start was vital. Johan went on a couple
of early runs to worry the Juventus defence, then
watched as a long cross looped towards the back post
and Johnny jumped highest. Johan wasn't even in the
box, but he felt himself move his head as if he was the
one heading the ball.

Johnny's header was perfectly placed, lobbing the
Juventus keeper and dropping under the crossbar.
Ajax were ahead!

That one goal was enough, and the Juventus players slumped to the ground at the final whistle. Johan and his teammates were already hugging each other and running towards the Ajax subs, coaches and fans.

'Three in a row!' Johan screamed.

'We're the Kings of Europe again!' Johnny yelled.

As the party carried on around him, Johan went to check on the Juventus players. He could sympathise with how they were probably feeling. When one of them asked to swap shirts, Johan couldn't say no.

But then he remembered he would need to wear a shirt to collect the trophy, and he wasn't going to get his Ajax shirt back now. So he put on the Juventus shirt he was holding. It felt a bit strange to be wearing another team's shirt for the ceremony, but none of that mattered when the trophy appeared just yards away from him.

Johan proudly lifted it into the air. What a night for Ajax! What a moment for Dutch football!

By the time the players got back to the dressing room, he was walking very slowly and dreaming of just getting into bed. He was exhausted.

The European Cup wasn't the only trophy that Johan was refusing to let out of his grip. A few weeks later, he was announced as the Ballon D'Or winner for the third year in a row.

But, as Johan would soon find out, these successes were really the calm before the storm.

CHAPTER 18

THE VOTE

1965–1973 – what a glorious eight years it had been for Ajax, winning six Dutch league titles and lifting three European cups in a row. The whole football world had fallen in love with the way they played the game, and this squad was still young enough to stay at the top for a long time too.

But a tense preseason would change everything.

Johan felt well rested when he arrived for the first training session. He was joking with a few of his teammates and thinking about new goals for the season ahead. Could they really win a fourth European Cup in a row?

But Coach Kovács had moved on, replaced by

George Knobel, and Johan sensed this was another fresh start at Ajax. That put some doubts in his mind. It had been hard enough to adjust to life without Coach Michels, and Johan had seen some warning signs last season even while they were winning trophies again.

'I don't know if this can last,' he remembered telling Henny last season. 'We're just not as connected and focused without Coach Michels. At some point, it's going to cost us.'

So, Coach Knobel was walking into a difficult situation, with some strong feelings bubbling below the surface. It got worse when he introduced himself to the players and explained that one of his first jobs was to choose a team captain.

Johan looked up, confused. What did he mean? Johan was the Ajax captain. He had just led the club to more trophies.

But Piet was another candidate, and he had captained the team in the 1971–72 season. Coach Knobel decided the only fair option was to have a vote.

'It's unbelievable,' Johan told Danny that night.

'I tried to talk to Coach Knobel again after training, but he won't change his mind. This shouldn't be a popularity contest!'

'Let's see what happens,' she said, gently. 'Don't forget, a lot of these players are your friends.'

'I hope you're right,' he replied, leaving the house for some fresh air.

Johan was still fuming, but he waited patiently for the results. Suddenly, he was doubting himself, though. Did his teammates think he was the wrong man to wear the captain's armband? Didn't all their years together chasing trophies count for something?

The results confirmed his worst fears. His teammates had made their feelings clear. Johan had lost the vote, and Piet would be the Ajax captain.

Johan was stunned. How could this be happening? Maybe his teammates thought he had received too much of the attention. Maybe they were jealous of his individual awards. Maybe he would never know the real reasons.

But it all seemed so unfair. He didn't ask for special treatment or extra attention – and he only yelled at his teammates to try to encourage them and make sure standards didn't slip at the club.

'I can't stay here!' he told Danny on the phone from the main training ground building. 'I need to leave.'

'Yes, of course – come home!' Danny said.

'No, I mean I need to leave Ajax,' he answered. 'This whole situation is all wrong.'

Johan could hardly believe he was saying those words out loud. He had joined the Ajax youth team as a ten-year-old and had never pictured himself playing for anyone else.

For the next few days, Johan thought about the situation over and over again. But how could he just go back to training as if nothing had happened? How could he walk into the dressing room and sit next to the other players? Johan just didn't feel welcome at Ajax anymore. There was really nothing left to say.

'If you're sure, we can call my dad and start the discussions with Ajax,' Danny said at last. Johan nodded. He had made up his mind.

When he heard about a possible transfer to Barcelona to reunite with Coach Michels, Johan jumped at the chance. That sounded like the ideal place to get his football joy back.

It was all happening so fast, but every bone in Johan's body was telling him that this was the right thing to do.

CHAPTER 19

BARCELONA BRILLIANCE: PART 1

'That's Cruyff!' one voice shouted.

'Hey, Johan!' called another. 'Welcome to Barcelona!'

Johan slowed down his morning jog to turn and wave. It was usually quiet on the beach at this time of day, but he had already learned that football doesn't really sleep in Barcelona.

He and Danny were enjoying everything about their new city – the restaurants, the weather and the relaxed lifestyle. After all the emotions when he left Ajax, Johan felt energised again, and he was still shocked by how many fans had waited for hours at the airport to welcome him.

'This is the start of a new era for Barcelona,' the club proudly announced when Johan arrived in Spain in August 1973. 'Cruyff is going to lead us back to the top!'

'Well, now I really have to play well!' Johan joked as reporters crowded around him. 'Don't worry. I'll be ready!'

He couldn't wait to start showing his talent on the pitch, but delays got in the way. Johan needed permission from the Roayl Dutch Football Association before he could play for a new team, and that led to long meetings as everyone tried to agree on a solution.

It was like a cruel trick. Johan went through all the training sessions with Coach Michels and his new teammates, but then he couldn't play in the matches. The pressure grew when Barcelona got off to a bad start without him, dropping to near the bottom of the table.

After reading another angry match report, Johan closed the newspaper and sighed. He was running out of patience. He just wanted to be out there on the pitch for Barcelona, doing what he did best: creating magic and winning games.

Finally, he got the approval to play, and the buzz began for his league debut against Granada.

'I feel bad for Granada,' said Juan Carlos, one of the Barcelona defenders. 'You're about to be unleashed and I doubt they're ready for it!'

Johan laughed. He actually felt quite calm. There was no point dwelling on the games he had missed or trying too hard to make a good first impression. The goals and assists would come – as long as he played the right way. He felt a shiver of excitement as he put on the purple-and-blue Barcelona shirt and tied his laces.

'Don't forget these,' Coach Michels said, handing Johan his shin pads. 'You might need them today if you're embarrassing their defenders!'

'They'll have to catch me first!' Johan answered, grinning.

Stepping out of the tunnel and onto the pitch at last, Johan had never heard a crowd make so much noise. 'Here we go!' he said, soaking up the applause and staring at the rows of fans that seemed to stretch all the way to the horizon.

Now he just needed to give them all something to cheer about. Johan could tell he was going to get lots of scoring chances in this Barcelona team, and he knew exactly what Coach Michels was expecting from him.

When the ball dropped to him just outside the penalty, he unleashed a rocket with his right foot. A defender blocked it, but it rebounded straight back to Johan. 'No problem, I'll try the left foot now,' he decided.

This time, he hit the shot even harder, and it flew past the goalkeeper and into the top corner.

Goooooooooooooooooooooooaaaaaaaaaaaaaaaaaaaa aaaaaaalllllllllllllllllllllllllllll!

The noise in the stadium was so loud that Johan couldn't even hear what his teammates were saying when they ran over to congratulate him. He added a second goal on the way to a 4–0 win, and his spark sent Barcelona on a winning run. There was a sudden change in the dressing room. They believed they could beat anyone.

'We're on a roll now!' said Hugo Sotil, who played up front with Johan.

'The rest of the league better watch out!' called
Juan Manuel Asensi, who was playing well in midfield.

Johan knew the biggest game of the season would
be away to rivals Real Madrid – and he was looking
forward to it.

'It's going to get loud out there, so keep your heads
and be prepared for a battle,' Coach Michels told the
players. 'Don't fall for their tricks.'

'We can win this,' Johan added. 'There's no better
message than beating them here at the Bernabéu.'

As Johan did a few last warm-up exercises, Coach
Michels appeared next to him on the touchline.
'Lead the way and the rest of the team will follow
you,' he said, patting Johan on the back. 'It's your
time to shine.'

Johan set the example with some early runs. He
called for the ball, sensed no defender behind him and
turned with it. His only thought was to dribble forward
and push Real Madrid back. Soon two or three white
Real shirts were trying to keep up with Johan, and that
opened up some space for everyone else.

Johan had to deal with kicks and pushes, but he

wasn't going to react. That's what the defenders wanted. The game would be much easier for them if Johan lashed out and got a red card.

Instead, he let his feet do the talking. After Asensi put Barcelona ahead, Johan took over. He controlled a pass, skipped past one defender, darted past another and held off a third, all while somehow keeping his balance and remembering where the goal was.

As the Real Madrid fans gasped in panic, Johan fired a low shot past the keeper.

Goooooooooooooooooooooooaaaaaaaaaaaaaaaaaaaa aaaaaaalllllllllllllllllllllllllllll!

'Whoa, how did you do that?!' Asensi shouted, rushing over to celebrate.

The Barcelona players were enjoying themselves now, and Johan was at the centre of every move. His through ball sent Juan Carlos clear for another goal, and they stunned the Bernabéu with a 5–0 win.

'This man is a magician!' Asensi said, hugging Johan as they headed for the team bus.

There was no stopping Barcelona now. They swept clear at the top of the table and, just ten months after joining the club, Johan was a Spanish league champion. He couldn't have wished for a better start.

The whole city seemed to have come together for one long party. Johan loved seeing all the happy faces, but he couldn't turn off his football brain yet. His next test was just weeks away.

CHAPTER 20

WORLD CUP WIZARD

International games with his Dutch teammates had become tenser since Johan's move to Barcelona, but everyone agreed that the 1974 World Cup was bigger than any awkward moments in the past.

The Netherlands had a great chance to lift the trophy for the first time, and Johan knew he had something to prove too. There had been lots of stories after his Ajax exit, but now it was all about the football.

In a funny twist, Johan was named captain for the World Cup, with Coach Michels calling the shots for the Netherlands. Could Johan lead his country on a tournament run?

As the squad arrived in Germany, that was the only

question that mattered. The Netherlands were drawn in Group 3 with Sweden, Bulgaria and Uruguay, and Johan was determined to make a fast start.

He sat with Johnny and Arie after one training session, feeling confident and counting the hours until the real games began.

'Dutch teams have had a pretty good run lately and we've all played in lots of big games,' Johan said, wiping sweat from his forehead.

'We can beat anyone if we play our best,' Arie replied.

'We're going to score lots of goals,' Johan added, smiling. 'I'm sure of that.'

Coach Michels was bringing his Total Football approach to the Netherlands team, and that meant lots of freedom for the attackers to drift around the pitch. A 2–0 win over Uruguay was a strong start, and Johan provided the main highlight in a 0–0 draw with Sweden by unleashing the 'Cruyff Turn', a breathtaking piece of skill.

Johan was in dazzling form again when the Dutch faced Bulgaria and were able to finish top of the opening group. His mazy run won an early penalty in a 4–1 win.

'We're playing well!' Coach Michels said, echoing Johan's own thoughts about the first three games. 'But we've got to be ready for tougher tests ahead.'

As the second group stage started, Johan was still looking for his first goal of the tournament, but he wouldn't have to wait much longer. Against Argentina, Johan was on the move as soon as the Netherlands won the ball back. He timed his run perfectly as the defenders looked for an offside flag.

There was no one around him, but Johan still had to control the floated pass. He watched the ball carefully, cushioned it with his right foot and dodged the Argentina keeper, who came flying off his line.

'Don't fall! Don't fall!' he told himself, as he tried to keep his balance. He stumbled a little but still had time to poke the ball into the empty net. 1–0!

Gooooooooooooooooooooooooaaaaaaaaaaaaaaaaaaaa aaaaaaalllllllllllllllllllllllllll!

Then Johan popped up on the left wing, dribbled forward and whipped in a brilliant cross. It was perfectly placed for Johnny to head the ball in.

Johan wasn't done yet though. He was lurking when a rebound pinged out towards the edge of the box. Without even needing a first touch to control the ball, he arrowed a shot into the bottom corner. 4–0!

Goooooooooooooooooooooooooaaaaaaaaaaaaaaaaaaaa aaaaaaalllllllllllllllllllllllllllll!

It was total domination, and Johan could hear the Dutch fans singing in the crowd.

Now they just had to beat Brazil, the defending World Cup champions, to clinch a place in the final. They didn't have Pelé this time, but it was still a strong Brazilian team. Even so, Johan and his teammates were sharper and created better chances. They just couldn't find the finishing touch.

Then Johan broke free on the right wing. He clipped a pass through to Neeskens, who floated a shot over the keeper. 1–0!

Neeskens raced over to Johan, arms out wide, and jumped into his arms. 'What a pass!' he shouted.

Further gaps appeared and the Netherlands attacked down the left wing. Johan sensed a chance and sprinted up in support. The cross flew into the box, and he steered a thumping first-time shot into the net. 2–0!

Gooooooooooooooooooooooooaaaaaaaaaaaaaaaaaaa aaaaaaalllllllllllllllllllllllllllllll!

'World Cup final, here we come!' Johan shouted, punching the air and thinking about all the fans back home watching the game.

But now they would face West Germany in the final.

'This is our chance to be heroes forever with one more special performance!' Johan said as the dressing room got quieter and quieter. Everyone else was thinking similar thoughts and trying to keep their nerves under control.

Johan was even more pumped up after the national anthem. 'Let's go!!' he yelled, as he stepped forward for the kick-off. The whistle blew and he passed the ball back to Neeskens. Game on!

That simple pass turned out to be the start of a sweeping attack. The Netherlands moved the ball around the pitch with fifteen passes straight from the kick-off, before Johan surged forward. A German tackle was a second too late, tripping him in the box. Penalty!

'West Germany haven't even touched the ball yet!' Johan thought, while watching Neeskens step forward for the penalty.

Neeskens made no mistake, scoring the penalty and stunning the home crowd. Just for a minute, Johan soaked it all in. The Netherlands were ahead in the World Cup final!

But little by little, the game slipped away. West Germany turned the game around to take a 2–1 lead, and Johan was so tightly marked that he couldn't drag the Netherlands back into the match this time.

As the West Germany players hugged and waved to the cheering crowd, Johan had a sick feeling in his stomach. This loss was going to sting for a long time.

At first, a runners-up medal felt like a disappointment, but Johan had to remember that there had been so many special World Cup moments over the last few weeks. The Netherlands had gained so many new fans around the world, and that made him happy.

CHAPTER 21

MISSING OUT

Johan's debut season at Barcelona had felt like the start of a dominant run. But he soon saw there were no guarantees. There were lots of other great teams in the Spanish league, and Real Madrid, Real Zaragoza and Atlético Madrid were all ready to take their crown.

Something just wasn't clicking for Barcelona like it had clicked in that first year, and the results began to slip. Johan couldn't really explain it. Sure, he regularly had two defenders following him around the pitch, but that was nothing new really. Barcelona still had some brilliant wins, but the performances weren't consistent enough. That was the harsh truth – and a pattern developed over the next few years.

Third place in 1975,
Second place in 1976...

Johan felt the frustration building. It was an unfamiliar feeling to fall short like this, and he could feel the impatience in the crowd. Barcelona tried to shake things up – with different coaches, different styles and different players. But they couldn't recapture the magic of their 1974 title run. With the pressure mounting, arguments in training became more common.

In some ways, it was a relief for Johan to escape for Euro 1976. 'This is the chance to end my trophy drought,' he thought to himself when he met up with his Dutch teammates. It was nice to have a new target to focus on, and there was a quiet confidence in the squad.

The European Championships format had just four teams involved at this final stage, and Johan was confident. The Netherlands had learned from their World Cup final disappointment, and he liked their chances of beating Czechoslovakia, their semi-final opponents.

'This is our time!' Johan shouted as they left the dressing room. 'Let's go!'

But the game plan fell apart in the first minute, with a yellow card for Johan. He couldn't believe it. He put his hands over his face – he would be suspended for the final even if the Netherlands got there.

'Aaaaaargh!' he yelled, while the rain poured down.

With mud spreading everywhere, there wasn't much chance of Total Football here. Johan wasn't at his best, and Czechoslovakia hung on to win 3–1 in extra-time. He was stunned as he trudged off the pitch. He had never even considered the possibility of losing.

Despite the setbacks, Johan never gave up. Back at Barcelona, he kept up his high standards, working hard in training and trying to turn things around. He still had a strong team around him, including Asensi, Netherlands teammate Neeskens and Spanish star Carles Rexach.

'We just need a little luck to go our way,' Johan said during training, while he and Neeskens swept long passes back and forth. 'That might be all it takes.'

When Barcelona reached the 1978 Spanish Cup
final, Johan knew this could be his last chance
for another trophy in Spain. Wearing the captain's
armband, he led by example in a 3–1 win, and he
couldn't stop grinning when he stepped up to receive
the cup. It felt amazing to end the trophy drought.

'That's more like it!' he shouted, hugging Carles.
'That looked like the real Barcelona today!'

'Well, you got things started for us,' replied Carles,
who had scored two of the goals. 'It was your run
that won us the early penalty, and we were on top
after that.'

The celebrations went on late into the night, with
music and singing and dancing. On other nights,
Johan might have made an excuse to leave the
party early. But that night, he wanted to enjoy it all.
Everything else could wait.

Not long after, the Dutch football association
wanted to know whether Johan would be available
for the 1978 World Cup, which was being held in
Argentina. He would have loved another chance
on that kind of stage to build on the Netherlands'

incredible show in 1974, but factors outside football made that impossible for Johan.

After a major scare for his family at their home in Barcelona, Johan decided he couldn't leave for the tournament. He would just be worrying all the time about whether they were safe. So, he put his family first and cheered on the team from the sofa. Some things were simply more important than football.

CHAPTER 22

SIGNING UP FOR 'SOCCER'

So, what's next?' Danny asked Johan during their walk in the park.

'I'm thinking it might be time to retire,' he said. 'I've had so many great years, and maybe it's better to walk away while my body still feels good.'

Danny raised an eyebrow. It was hard to imagine Johan shifting into a life without football.

'Well, I mean, that's one option, anyway,' he added, sensing she had her doubts.

Johan was still thinking about his next move when he got a phone call. It was bad news. A business deal had fallen apart, and Johan had lost a lot of money.

Suddenly, it was hard to think about retirement.

'On second thoughts, maybe I'll play for a few more years!' he told Danny, trying to make her smile. The situation certainly wasn't funny – but for a second, they both laughed.

Then, in 1979, a new offer landed on his desk, giving him an opportunity he had never even thought about. The North American Soccer League was always looking for top players to move over to the United States. Pelé had given the league a bump in popularity and attracted other stars to join him. Now they wanted Johan to become the latest big-name signing.

'What do you think?' Johan asked Danny, while they looked at the details.

'Are these team names real?' Danny said laughing. 'The Tampa Bay Rowdies? The California Surf?'

'I think so!' Johan answered. 'The league is still quite new, but this could be a really fun adventure for the whole family.'

Before he knew it, Johan was on a plane, flying first to New York for a few friendlies with the New York Cosmos, and then to Los Angeles to join the

Los Angeles Aztecs and his good friend Coach Michels.

'The two friendlies in New York were on astroturf pitches,' Johan told Coach Michels. 'I'm not sure I can get through a whole season on those.'

'Well, don't worry about that,' Coach Michels replied. 'We've got a beautiful grass pitch here. Your knees will thank you!'

When Johan was dropped off at the Los Angeles Aztecs' home pitch, he was surprised to see Coach Michels and a few other coaches waiting for him, with one even holding a fresh team kit.

'Hi Coach,' Johan said. 'I wasn't expecting a tour on my first day!'

Coach Michels smiled back at him. 'Feeling fresh after the flight?'

'Yeah, not bad,' Johan said, wondering why Coach Michels was looking so suspicious.

'Excellent. We've got a game tonight, and this kit should be the right size.'

'I'm playing today?!' Johan asked, caught by surprise. 'I thought you were joking about that!'

He hadn't even met his teammates or joined a single training session. But Coach Michels wasn't worried.

Johan still couldn't believe this was happening as he walked into the changing room. His teammates gave him a warm welcome, though he couldn't tell if some of them were completely star-struck or a bit unsure about why he was there. Johan was determined to show that this wasn't just a paid holiday. As always, he was serious about winning.

It turned out that Johan didn't really need a training session before making his Aztecs debut. He was often at his best when he had the freedom to get creative on the pitch, and that's exactly what Coach Michels gave him.

'I won't play you for long tonight, but the crowd are going to go wild when they see you're here,' Coach Michels said. 'Just get us a lead to defend.'

Johan nodded. With one of his first touches, he created space and rocketed a shot past the keeper.

Goooooooooooooooooooooooooaaaaaaaaaaaaaaaaaaaaaa aaaaaaallllllllllllllllllllllllllllll!

His new teammates crowded round him. Johan still

didn't know most of their names, but they definitely knew his.

After seven minutes, he had scored two goals and set up another. 'Is that what you had in mind?' he called to Coach Michels with a wink.

'I think we might be pretty good this year!' joked one of the Los Angeles defenders.

'Yeah, all we've been missing is a Ballon d'Or winner!' another teammate teased.

All the spotlight was on Johan after the game. He was used to that, but he had learned from his Ajax experience, and he tried to praise his teammates whenever he could.

Though the NASL wasn't at the same standard as the Dutch league or the Spanish league, it was a perfect chance for Johan to entertain. He wowed the fans with runs where the ball seemed to be stuck to his boot. None of the defenders had a chance of taking it from him.

Life in Los Angeles suited Johan too. He could walk around in the sunshine with his family without many people knowing who he was. It was a city of film stars and musicians. It wasn't unusual to see a celebrity at a restaurant or in the street.

The Aztecs qualified for the NASL playoffs, and Johan had another moment of magic ready for the next game. Against the Washington Diplomats, he got the ball just inside his own half and the defenders were already backing off.

Johan dribbled forward, on and on until a defender finally rushed at him. With a quick drop of the shoulder, he skipped past a weak tackle, then weaved past two more defenders, who ran into each other and ended up on the floor.

He glanced up to see where the keeper was, then curled a shot into the corner of the net.

Gooooooooooooooooooooooooooaaaaaaaaaaaaaaaaaaaa aaaaaaallllllllllllllllllllllllllll!

The whole stadium gasped. It was an instant highlight.

At the end of a memorable season, the Aztecs missed out on the NASL trophy, but Johan was named Most Valuable Player, and he was beginning to think the move to Los Angeles had been a brilliant idea.

CHAPTER 23

WASHINGTON WHIRLWIND

Yet the Cruyffs were soon coming up with a new plan. After that first season, the Aztecs went in a different direction, focusing on Mexican players, and that meant Johan and his big contract had to go.

Before Johan could even consider a return to Europe, the Washington Diplomats swooped in. They sent senior staff to Los Angeles and made a persuasive presentation.

'We want to put our club on the soccer map,' they explained. 'That means building a better team that the fans will really connect with. Come to Washington and be our star man.'

In early 1980, Johan signed with the Diplomats,

but he had forgotten one very important detail. In Los Angeles, he was a perfect fit for what Coach Michels wanted to do. In Washington, the system was very different.

'Whack it away!' the coaches yelled in practice, encouraging the defenders to punt the ball down the field.

Johan put his hands on his hips. The latest long ball had gone nowhere near him. 'We don't have to do that every time,' he told the coaches. 'What about a simple pass into midfield instead?'

But that wasn't the way the Diplomats played. Johan hadn't expected Total Football, but he assumed there would be a few passing moves. His attempts to give advice to his teammates often ended up in arguments rather than improvements.

Johan was confused. He was filming TV programmes about 'soccer' – the rules, the skills, the tactics. But some of his own teammates weren't even following his instructions.

'Just focus on what you can control,' Danny suggested.

Johan nodded. 'You're right,' he said. 'For the rest of this season, I'm going to put on my own show.'

Sure enough, the old Johan dribbling runs were back in the next game. He was having fun again in training too, leaving the other players speechless with the way he could put curl and swerve on his shots.

'Wow, show me how you do that!' called Bob, one of the team's defenders, after Johan had bent a shot effortlessly into the top corner from well outside the box.

Johan placed a ball in front of Bob, then took three steps back.

'You've got to make the connection with the outside of your boot,' he explained, pointing to his own foot. 'That's what puts the swerve on the shot. Try it.'

Bob's first and second attempts sliced wide of the goal, but his third effort was much better.

'That's it!' Johan said, clapping. 'Sometimes that's the best technique. Defenders are in position to block a normal shot, but this catches them out.'

Johan saved his best moment for a game against Seattle. He started dribbling at walking pace, just waiting to see how his markers would react. Then he spotted a little gap and burst between them, keeping the ball close to him.

Now he had built up some speed, and he surged into the penalty area. The Seattle defenders were terrified about fouling him, so Johan raced through and fired a shot past the keeper's dive and into the net.

Goooooooooooooooooooooooooaaaaaaaaaaaaaaaaaaa aaaaaaalllllllllllllllllllllllllllllll!

'What a run!' the commentators screamed. 'Cruyff made it look so easy!'

Johan and the Diplomats crashed out of the playoffs, losing to the Aztecs after a late goal was ruled out, but an even bigger disappointment was around the corner. The message was brief and shocking: The Diplomats had run out of money.

'What's going on?' Johan asked. When he found out more, it was clear that this version of the team in Washington was over. It was another reminder that the sport had a long way to go in the United States.

Once again, Johan suddenly had big, unexpected decisions to make. He had no regrets about his NASL experience but, after a brief spell at Levante in Spain and a few more games back in Washington, Johan knew it was time to go home.

Whenever he thought about Ajax, it was usually the European Cup memories that appeared first. But Johan still regretted the way things had ended. This was the club that he had loved since he was a little boy, and he needed to write a new ending to that story.

CHAPTER 24

UNFINISHED BUSINESS

When a stadium was packed with fans, it was so noisy and electric. Lamine usually had to yell just so a teammate could hear him five yards away.

'I'm coming home!' Johan told his family and friends. 'And I'll be back at Ajax!'

There was a flurry of emotions in the air when Johan returned to Amsterdam. It was 1980. Ajax were a different club compared to Johan's glory years there, but they still had great players and they had won the 1979–80 title.

Seeing the red-and-white Ajax scarves and the familiar home dressing room, so many memories came rushing back to Johan as he answered reporters' questions and prepared for the new season.

At first, he was just there as an advisor, sitting in the crowd and taking notes. After each game, he prepared reports about what he thought was working well on the pitch and where the team could improve. If he saw something really important, he even hurried down the stairs at half-time to make the suggestion to the Ajax manager.

But being so close to the action left Johan wanting more. As he watched the games, he kept thinking about what he would do in certain situations. What kind of pass would he have played? What would he have done in a one-on-one with the keeper?

The more he thought about it, the more he wanted to be at the centre of the action again. So, before the 1981–82 season, he made a new agreement with Ajax. He was ready to return as a player.

'Are you sure about this?' one reporter asked.

'I've still got some magic left in me,' Johan replied. 'As long as I can still run, I want to help Ajax become champions again.'

This was going to be a different version of Johan,

though. He couldn't dribble past defenders quite so easily now, but he could still see passes that no one else on the pitch could see, and he loved being a leader for young players like Marco van Basten and Frank Rijkaard.

'It's making me feel younger!' Johan told the coaches. 'These young kids are sprinting all over the pitch just like I used to.'

'Don't worry, we're happy doing the running for you, Grandpa,' Frank joked, appearing in the doorway.

With Johan helping out in lots of different positions, Ajax scored 117 goals in 34 games on the way to the 1981–82 title, and he felt great to be part of a brilliant, attacking team again. He even scored a few screamers himself, and he rolled his eyes when his younger teammates looked surprised.

'I was scoring goals like that before you were even born,' Johan said, grinning. 'You can ask anyone!'

He was always working on new ways to entertain the fans too. When Ajax won a penalty against Helmond, Johan saw an opportunity for a cheeky trick and whispered in the ear of his teammate Jesper Olsen.

Johan put the ball on the spot and stepped back, waiting for the goalkeeper to get into position. Then he started his run-up. But instead of firing a shot, he tapped the ball forward to Jesper, who was running in from the edge of the box. Jesper passed it back to Johan for a simple tap-in.

Goooooooooooooooooooooooaaaaaaaaaaaaaaaaaaaa aaaaaaalllllllllllllllllllllllllllll!

The fans shrieked, and the Helmond players complained to the referee, but it was all within the rules. Johan high-fived Jesper as they jogged back to the halfway line. Not for the first time, Johan had left most of his teammates speechless.

Best of all, Johan could feel the fans' passion again. Ajax even moved some of their home matches to the Olympic Stadium because so many people wanted a ticket to see the team – and Johan still got the loudest cheers.

As he prepared for another trophy celebration, he was excited to share this one with the whole family.

Ajax had won the 1982–83 Dutch league and cup double, and the whole city was ready to celebrate its football heroes.

'What a day!' Johan said, looking out at all the Ajax fans. There were rows of people on the pavements and kids on their parents' shoulders. 'I was a kid like that once. The Ajax team were like a part of my family.'

'Well, that's the next generation right there,' one of the Ajax coaches replied. 'We're keeping the winning tradition going.'

Johan nodded and smiled. 'I hope so!' he said.

CHAPTER 25

RALLYING THE RIVALS

Johan had never imagined playing for another Dutch team. Ajax had been his first love, and that meant every other club in the Netherlands was a rival.

But as his Ajax contract ended, in 1983, it was clear that the club was ready to move on without him. That meant he had another hard decision to make. If he wanted to play next season, Johan needed to find another club.

When Feyenoord approached him, Johan's first instinct was to hesitate. Could he really sign for a team that he had battled for so many years in the Dutch league? But he had fewer doubts after talking to Feyenoord's directors and manager Thijs Libregts.

'We still believe you're one of the best players in the league,' Coach Libregts said. 'Bring that talent to Feyenoord and we're ready to make a run.'

Johan grinned. It felt good that Feyenoord still saw him as a star.

He picked up a pen to sign the contract, but he did so knowing there would be some harsh reactions to the news. He might have to win over the Feyenoord fans at first, and probably some of the senior players too, but he was determined to make this a successful season.

That motivation carried over into the summer. Johan wasn't going to wait until the preseason sessions to work on his fitness. He filled his days with tennis, jogging and long walks. He was 36 years old but he wanted to be able to match the 26-year-olds.

The early signs weren't good, though. When Feyenoord lost 8–2 to Ajax, the reaction was predictable. Johan was part of Ajax's past – whereas van Basten was Ajax's future. There were endless jokes and headlines.

Johan heard it all, but it was going to take more

than one bad afternoon to dent his confidence.

'It's one game, guys,' Johan said in the dressing room. 'We lost. It doesn't matter if it was 1–0 or 8–2. We've just got to focus on the next match. We'll be fine.'

Feyenoord followed his lead and didn't look back. Johan quickly formed a deadly partnership with young star Ruud Gullit, and the wins started to pile up.

'We make a pretty good team,' Ruud joked, patting Johan on the back. 'The guy with great hair… and Johan.'

Feyenoord were especially unstoppable at home as the goals flew in.

7–2 against HFC Haarlem,

5–2 against AZ Alkmaar,

5–2 against Roda…

They even knocked Ajax out of the Dutch cup. But the game everyone was talking about was the league rematch against Ajax.

Johan tried not to overthink it. The drama with Ajax was in the past. Of course, he wanted to play well, but winning the game was the most important thing. Feyenoord were chasing a league title, and he wouldn't let himself get distracted by anything else.

Ruud curled in a stunning free kick to put Feyenoord ahead, then Johan had his big moment. The Ajax keeper saved a powerful header, but the rebound fell to Johan. He couldn't believe his luck! He drilled the ball into the net with his left foot.

Goooooooooooooooooooooooooaaaaaaaaaaaaaaaaaaa aaaaaaallllllllllllllllllllllllllll!

Johan jumped in the air, feeling all kinds of emotions, and his teammates buried him in hugs. They knew it was a big deal for him to score against Ajax. A lot of things had been said about Johan that season, and he was answering in the best possible way. Feyenoord won 4–1 to get a little payback for the bad loss earlier in the season, and no one was mocking Johan now.

A few months later, he was standing for photos in front of the Dutch league and cup trophies. It was such a special way to end that unexpected season of 1983–84, but Johan's body was sending him a message. All the aches and pains had slowed him down, and it took a big effort just to get out of bed after games.

'Daddy, are you okay?' asked Susila, his youngest daughter, as Johan limped down the stairs one morning. She looked concerned to see him in pain, and that really made him think. Johan had always wanted to finish his career on a high note. This felt like the right moment.

'It's time,' he told Danny as they sat on the beach that summer. 'It's been an unbelievable ride, and I'm ready to hang up my boots now.'

CHAPTER 26

FROM THE FIELD TO THE DUGOUT

There was no way Johan was just going to sit at home when he retired. He and Danny were too active for that. Instead, it was the freedom of having no schedule that excited him. Johan still went to watch plenty of Dutch league games – sometimes at Ajax, sometimes in other cities – and his brain was always busy assessing what he saw.

The more Johan watched, the more interested he became in a coaching job – and once again, it brought him back to Ajax, where he was named Technical Director and would oversee the first team squad.

His relationship with Ajax had been a wild

rollercoaster ride over the years, but he and Danny agreed that it was time to move past that. Amsterdam still felt like home, and Johan was excited for his children to grow up there.

He wasn't a qualified coach yet, but Johan had always loved thinking about the tactical side of football, and he surrounded himself with experienced coaches to run the training sessions. He liked the puzzle of comparing different formations and different styles to create the game plan for each opponent. It was something he had done ever since his first conversations with Coach Michels.

He also had a clear idea of how he wanted his team to play – his own version of Total Football – and now he just needed enough time on the training ground to put the plan together.

'Some people might say that our only job is to win games,' Johan told his players at the start of his first season as coach. 'But, to me, we've got two jobs – winning games and entertaining the fans. That's the way I want us to play. We're going to be bold, and we're going to win trophies!'

The early signs looked promising, and it didn't take long for Johan to see that management suited him, even though he had been teammates with some of the Ajax players just a few years ago, including Marco and Frank.

'I had a feeling you'd like being the boss!' Danny teased.

His first home game in charge was a day he would never forget. He stepped out of the tunnel after a familiar walk from the dressing room, but this time his path was straight to the dugout.

'Cruyff! Cruyff! Cruyff!'

As the fans chanted his name, Johan turned and waved. He felt the hairs on his arms standing on end, confirming in his mind that taking this job was the right decision.

There were lots of smiles in the Ajax dressing room, but Johan knew how important it was to win some trophies to keep the momentum going. When they won the Dutch Cup in 1986, with two goals from Marco in extra-time, Johan was leaping around on the touchline.

The next season, he was the mastermind for an even better season, in which Ajax defended the Dutch Cup and added the European Cup Winners' Cup. That European success was another huge step for such a young squad, and Johan could see that the players were still a little stunned as they celebrated with the trophy.

As usual, Johan was soon starting to think about the following season. He had plans for each of the players to help them improve, but the club had other ideas. Ajax sold Marco and missed out on some of Johan's favourite replacements. It left the whole team looking for answers.

'We can't waste this opportunity,' Johan said to himself when he heard the latest transfer news. 'We've got so many good young players, but we've got to make the right decisions to support them. If we do, this could be a real golden era for Ajax.'

Instead, things went downhill at an even faster pace, and Johan found himself back in the tense situations he had experienced before at Ajax. All he wanted was to focus on his coaching without interference, but there were new opinions to deal with every week. He just didn't have the patience or the energy for that anymore.

Even though he loved working with the players, Johan felt he had no choice now. For the third time in his life, he knew he needed to leave Ajax.

CHAPTER 27

BARCELONA BRILLIANCE: PART 2

When Barcelona were looking for a new manager in 1988, there was only one man on their wishlist: Johan.

And so, ten years after leaving the club as a player, now he found himself back at the Camp Nou with a big job to do. Barcelona had been through a difficult spell, but Johan was confident he could lead Barcelona back to the top, just like he did when he joined the club as a player.

'It's the right job at the right time,' he had said, as soon as he got the call.

Johan made it clear straight away that he was calling

the shots. With his old teammate Carles Rexach as his assistant manager, he felt ready to handle the gloomy mood in Barcelona.

'You'll be a hero if you can turn this around,' Carles told him. 'But there's a lot to fix here!'

Johan understand that. He would have to make some changes, but the talent was there. Within the first thirty minutes of his first training session, he saw enough potential to get excited about the season ahead, including England striker Gary Lineker.

'Remember how good our teams were back then?' Johan asked Carles after one training session. 'This team is going to be even better! It won't happen overnight, but we'll get there.'

The 1988–89 season was supposed to be a learning year, but Johan was aiming higher. Barcelona beat Sampdoria to lift the European Cup Winners' Cup, and the mood started to change. A year later, Barcelona won the Spanish Cup.

Slowly, he was bringing back the glory days and creating the kind of team that he believed could take over Spanish football. There were global stars all over the pitch now, from Michael Laudrup and Hristo Stoichkov to Ronald Koeman and Pep Guardiola, and Johan liked to join in the training games sometimes.

'He's still got it!' Ronald shouted after one of Johan's smooth flicks.

The Spanish league title was the target heading into the 1990–91 season, and Barcelona were off to a good start. But Johan woke up one morning and immediately didn't feel quite right. He felt a sharp pain in his chest and was rushed to the hospital.

Things got worse, and Johan was booked in for major heart surgery. When he woke up after the surgery, he was happy to see his family gathered around him – and then his next question was predictable.

'Did we win yesterday?' he asked, looking at his son Jordi, who had become a big Barcelona fan.

Danny laughed. 'It's nice to see you're still your usual self!' she said. 'And yes, Barcelona won!'

When Barcelona clinched the title by ten points that summer, Johan was cheered everywhere he went in the city. 'We're back!' he shouted, making the fans cheer even louder.

A year later, he led Barcelona into the 1992 European Cup Final – and again, it was Sampdoria standing in their way. These were the moments when Johan's experience as a player really helped him as a manager. He had been in these big games, he understood what the players were going through and he knew how to take the pressure off their shoulders.

When the players walked onto the pitch at Wembley, Johan felt the butterflies in his stomach. This was so much more nerve-wracking as a coach!

It was 0–0 after ninety minutes and Johan took a deep breath as he walked onto the pitch for another quick team-talk. There were still thirty more minutes to go, and maybe a penalty shootout too. He could feel the sweat rolling down his back as he loosened the collar of his shirt.

'No one said it was going to be easy,' Johan told the players, with a grin. 'You're doing a great job. Now we've got to dig even deeper. Do it for each other. Find that extra burst of energy. It'll all be worth it when you're holding the European Cup!'

Johan sat down on the bench again, but he was

jumping with his arms in the air when Ronald's
free kick rocketed into the net, deep in extra-time.
'Yeeeeeesss!!'

The Barcelona players rushed over to the corner
flag to celebrate, and Johan climbed over one of the
advertising boards around the edge of the pitch. He
wasn't sure where he was going, but he wanted to be
closer to the action. Surely that had to be the
winning goal.

'We've almost done it!' he whispered to himself
nervously.

After eight more nail-biting minutes, Johan heard
the final whistle, and he was wrapped in hugs
from the coaches and substitutes. Then he joined
the players on the pitch, savouring the familiar joy
of winning a big final. Together with winning the
Spanish league again, it had been an amazing year!

Johan had wondered if he would ever hold the
European Cup in his hands again. But there it was,
right in front of him – and he was back on top of the
football mountain.

CHAPTER 28

THE CRUYFF LEGACY

Johan won two more league titles with Barcelona, making it four in a row, but when his time as manager there came to an end after eight years, he decided to step back from football – and he mostly stuck to that promise. He now really just had two main goals in mind: spending more time with his family and making a difference with charity work.

One morning, in the summer of 1996, Johan's phone buzzed on the table next to him. He glanced over and saw the call was from Jordi. The next few minutes got him sitting on the edge of his seat. Jordi had just received an offer to sign for Manchester United.

Johan knew it hadn't been easy for Jordi, with all

the expectations of following in Johan's footsteps. But he had developed into a very good midfielder, and Johan was proud of his son's success. Retirement gave him more chances to follow Jordi's career and spend time with Danny, Chantal and Susila.

The Cruyff Foundation became one of his main projects, setting up kids with opportunities to play sport and exercise.

'If you can do something for someone else, you should,' Johan said, explaining why the foundation meant so much to him.

That was just the start, though. Johan also created the Cruyff Institute, giving sports management training to athletes, and the Cruyff Courts, which were new pitches across the country for kids to use. It was all designed to support the next generation of players – then and into the future.

Johan kept his strong ties to Barcelona too. Many years earlier, he had been one of the brains behind La Masia, the club's youth academy, and he was always interested to see how the team was doing.

But then, unfortunately, Johan's health started to

go downhill. A serious illness affected his lungs, and his family gathered around him in a hospital in Barcelona. He died in March 2016, at the age of sixty-eight, and tributes poured in from all over the world.

From Pelé: 'We have lost a great man. May we carry on his example of excellence. Johan Cruyff was a great player and coach. He leaves a very important legacy for our family of football.'

From Ruud Gullit: 'Thank you Johan for being my biggest inspiration and teacher. Thank you for paving the way for our generation and for putting the Netherlands on the map. Thank you for being you.'

And even from Jan Olsson, who would always be tied to Johan by the famous 'Cruyff Turn': 'I don't understand how he did it. Every day I think about football, I think about Johan Cruyff.'

As one of football's best players and greatest entertainers, Johan's achievements would never be forgotten – and his contributions to the game would live on forever.

Read on for a sneak preview of
another brilliant football story by
Matt and Tom Oldfield. . .

MARADONA

Available now!

CHAPTER 1

ARGENTINA'S WORLD CUP HERO

Mexico – 29 June 1986

Diego fixed the captain's armband on his sleeve and focused on glory. This had been his dream for as long as he could remember – to win the World Cup Final for his country, Argentina. In football, it didn't get any bigger or better than that.

'How are you feeling?' the manager Carlos Bilardo asked him in the dressing room. He was relying on his superstar, today more than ever.

'Ready,' Diego replied with a confident smile.

No one had ever doubted the talent in the

Argentina team. After all, they had Diego wearing the Number 10 shirt, the best and most expensive player in the world. Instead, it was the winning attitude that seemed to be missing.

Could they really go all the way and win it, just like they had at home in Argentina in 1978?

Or, with the pressure on, would they fall apart, just like they had in Spain in 1982?

That was the big question when the 1986 tournament began, and boy were Argentina answering it! South Korea, Bulgaria, Uruguay, England and Belgium – they had beaten them all. Under Diego's leadership, Argentina had been transformed from a squad of fighting misfits into a team with togetherness, strength and spirit.

Diego was in the best form of his life, but he couldn't win the World Cup on his own. Oscar Ruggeri and José Luis Cuciuffo in defence, Héctor Enrique and Jorge Burruchaga in midfield, Jorge Valdano in attack – they were all playing an important part in Argentina's success.

'Six down, one to go!' Diego kept reminding them

of their tally of victories as the final drew near. 'Come on, guys, we're so nearly there!'

The last team in their way was West Germany. Diego wasn't at all surprised to be facing them in the final; when it came to big tournaments, they always found a way to win.

'Not today, though,' he told his teammates before kick-off. 'This is our day, our World Cup!'

In the tunnel, the Argentina players shouted and beat their chests like a band of gorillas. Other teams had been frightened by this, but not West Germany. Their players weren't scared of anything. Diego and co. would have to beat them with their footballing skill instead.

As the two teams walked out onto the pitch in Mexico City, the 115,000 fans roared and waved their respective team's national flags: black, red and yellow for West Germany, and light blue and white for Argentina. Diego looked up at the rows and rows of blurred faces above. There were so many people waiting, hoping, expecting. He couldn't let his nation down, and he wouldn't. It was his duty to bring the World Cup home.

'Let's do this!' Diego clapped and cheered, looking along the line at his teammates.

When the game started, it soon became clear that West Germany's Lothar Matthäus was man-marking Diego, Argentina's danger man. Italy's Claudio Gentile had successfully stopped him back in 1982, but Diego was now older and wiser. Could he get the better of Matthäus when it mattered most? It wouldn't be easy. The German wasn't just a tough defender; he was also skilful and smart.

'You're not going anywhere,' Matthäus told him with an evil grin.

'We'll see about that!' Diego replied. He was desperate to grab another goal. What a tournament he was having. He'd scored two against England in the quarter-final – the 'Hand of God' and the 'Goal of the Century' – and then two against Belgium in the semi-final. A goal in the final would be the icing on the cake. It would prove once and for all that 1986 had been Diego's World Cup.

More importantly, however, he was desperate to

win the final. When José Luis Brown and Jorge Valdano put Argentina 2–0 up, Diego was just as excited as everyone else. He didn't need to be the national hero every time.

'Keep going!' Diego urged his teammates. 'Remember, West Germany never give up.'

He was right. First, Karl-Heinz Rummenigge tapped one in. 2–1! Then, Rudi Völler headed home. 2–2!

'Uh-oh,' Diego thought to himself. For the first time all tournament, he was scared. What if West Germany scored again and stole the World Cup away from them? Argentina needed to dig deep and find a winner from somewhere.

'Come on, they're tired!' Diego shouted. 'Let's finish them off before extra time!'

In the centre-circle, he had six West Germany players around him, but he didn't panic. Somehow, when he was on the ball, time seemed to stand still. In a flash, he spotted a gap and he spotted Jorge Burruchaga's run. Diego hit the pass first-time and 'Burru' sprinted into the penalty area and scored. 3–2 to Argentina!

'Yes, you did it!' Diego screamed with delight.

'No, we did it!' Burru corrected his incredible captain.

Argentina still had six minutes to hold on. Bilardo barked out frantic instructions on the touchline. 'No messing around! Mark up!'

Diego only knew one way to defend – attack. He linked up with the two Jorges one last time and stormed through the German defence. In the box, the keeper brought him down.

'Penalty!' Diego cried out, but the referee gave an earlier free kick instead. Argentina didn't mind – they were now seconds away from glory.

As West Germany launched one final ball upfield, Diego kept looking over at the referee, waiting for that whistle.

'Hurry up!' he muttered impatiently.

Finally, the referee raised his arms and blew. In that moment, Diego went crazy. He ran around, hugging everybody. 'We did it! We did it!' he shouted over and over again.

The Argentina fans invaded the pitch and soon Diego was at the centre of a big, chanting crowd.

Mar-a-Don-a! Mar-a-Don-a!

Vamos Vamos Argentina!

As he watched and listened to his nation's joy, Diego burst into tears. Winning the World Cup was the greatest achievement of his life. He was so proud of his team.

'Come on, let's go get our trophy!' Diego told them.

As he held the World Cup for the first time, his hands were shaking. He looked at it lovingly and then lifted it high. He kissed it passionately, and then lifted it high again. He didn't want to let go.

'Hey, don't be greedy!' Jorge Valdano teased. 'Share it around!'

The Argentina players had achieved their wildest dream. They were returning home as world champions.

Back down on the pitch, the crowd carried Diego on their shoulders for a lap of honour. There was no feeling like it – love, pride and joy all merged into one. He felt like a king, the King of Football and the King of Argentina.

Chitoro and Tota's son hadn't just become a star;

Diego had become his country's greatest star. He would go down in history. From the dirt tracks of Villa Fiorito, Diego was now Argentina's World Cup hero.

CHAPTER 2

VILLA FIORITO

The day of 30 October 1960 was bright and sunny in Villa Fiorito. For most of the local people, it was a Sunday like any other, filled with church, food and family time.

For the Maradonas, however, it was about to become a very busy Sunday indeed. Diego 'Chitoro' and Doña Tota already had four daughters and now their first son was about to be born. It would be another mouth to feed but they couldn't wait to welcome the new member of their family.

'Chitoro!' Tota called out, as she sat resting in a chair in the shade. She didn't panic at all. 'It's time!'

Her husband rushed around their tiny home,

collecting a few things to take to the Policlínico Evita Hospital in Lanús – clothes, blankets, toys. The family didn't have much but Chitoro wanted to make sure that his first son was as comfortable as possible.

'Right, let's go!' he said, carefully helping his wife up out of her chair.

'Wait,' Tota said suddenly.

Chitoro thought that it might be a false alarm, but in fact, something shiny had caught Tota's eye. 'What's that?' she asked, pointing.

Their eldest daughter, Ana Maria, brought the item over to her. It was a brooch in the shape of a star, with glass beads that glistened like diamonds.

Tota smiled. 'Could you pin it to my dress please, my darling?' she asked. 'It's a good sign. Our son – your brother – is going to be a star!'

Chitoro and Tota had every reason to hope for bigger and better things. Their family was one of the poorest families in Villa Fiorito, which was itself one of the poorest parts of Buenos Aires, Argentina's capital city.

Life was a constant struggle and sometimes, the family couldn't afford to eat. They lived in a small house with one small bedroom for the adults and one small bedroom for the children. The third room was where they cooked, ate and did everything except sleep. Every time it rained, the roof leaked.

The Maradonas had no running water in the house. Every day, they took it in turns to go to the tap down the street. They filled up big, heavy jugs to carry back for cooking, washing and drinking.

'Our children will grow up big and strong!' Chitoro liked to joke.

They hadn't always lived there in Fiorito, however. Chitoro and Tota were originally from the Corrientes Province in the north-east of the country. One day, they decided to move nearer to Buenos Aires, looking for better job opportunities.

Back home, Chitoro had been a boatman but in Fiorito, he worked as a bricklayer and a factory worker. He worked all day every day, but none of his jobs paid well. Tota stayed at home to look after their children, so it was up to him to earn enough money to put food on the table. That wasn't easy at all, especially now that there were seven of them.

'And boys eat more,' Tota warned her husband when they returned home from the hospital. 'Diego's got a very healthy appetite already!'

They had named their first son 'Diego' after his dad, and 'Armando', meaning 'soldier'. If he was really going to grow up to become a star, he had a fierce battle to fight. Growing up in Villa Fiorito was dangerous and difficult. There were so few jobs available that many kids in the neighbourhood were tempted into a life of crime. Diego, however, would be different. He was special.

'I mean, just look how much hair he's got already!' Tota laughed.

Chitoro and Tota were determined, and shared a belief that their son would be the one to help the family to escape from poverty.

Tota hoped that their son would grow up to be a kind and healthy person with a good, respectable job.

'Perhaps Diego will be an accountant,' she dreamt.

Chitoro hoped that their son would have opportunities that he never had growing up.

JOHAN CRUYFF

Ajax

🏆 Eredivisie (Dutch League): 1965–66, 1966–67, 1967–68, 1969–70, 1971–72, 1972–73, 1981–82, 1982–83

🏆 KNVB Cup: 1966–67, 1969–70, 1970–71, 1971–72, 1982–83

🏆 European Cup: 1970–71, 1971–72, 1972–73

🏆 European Super Cup: 1972

🏆 Intercontinental Cup: 1972

Barcelona
🏆 La Liga: 1973–74
🏆 Copa del Rey: 1977–78

Feyenoord
🏆 Eredivisie: 1983–84
🏆 KNVB Cup: 1983–84

Netherlands
🏆 FIFA World Cup Runner-up: 1974

Barcelona
🏆 La Liga: 1990–91, 1991–92, 1992–93, 1993–94
🏆 Copa del Rey: 1989–90
🏆 Supercopa de España: 1991, 1992, 1994
🏆 European Cup: 1991–92
🏆 European Cup Winners' Cup: 1988–89
🏆 European Super Cup: 1992

Individual
🏆 Ballon d'Or: 1971, 1973, 1974
🏆 Eredivisie top scorer: 1966–67, 1971–72

- Dutch Footballer of the Year: 1968, 1972, 1984
- Dutch Sportsman of the Year: 1973, 1974
- FIFA World Cup Golden Ball: 1974
- FIFA World Cup All-Star Team: 1974
- Don Balón Award for Best La Liga Foreign Player: 1977, 1978
- North American Soccer League MVP: 1979
- World Team of the 20th Century

CRUYFF

14 THE FACTS

NAME: Hendrik Johannes Cruyff

DATE OF BIRTH: 25 April 1947

PLACE OF BIRTH: Amsterdam

Age: Died in 2016, aged 68

NATIONALITY: Dutch

CURRENT CLUB: As a player – Ajax, Barcelona, Los Angeles Aztecs, Washington Diplomats, Feyenoord; As a manager – Ajax, Barcelona, Catalonia

POSITION: FW

THE STATS

Height (cm):	178
Club appearances:	713
Club goals:	400
Club trophies:	22
International appearances:	48
International goals:	33
International trophies:	0
BALLON D'ORS:	3

★ ★ ★ **HERO RATING: 94** ★ ★ ★

GREATEST MOMENTS

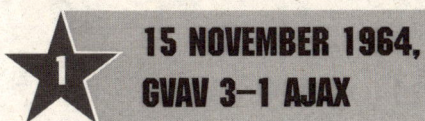

1 15 NOVEMBER 1964, GVAV 3–1 AJAX

It was a dream come true for Johan when he made his debut against GVAV, just seven years after joining the club's youth team. Playing alongside some of his childhood idols, he showed flashes of his football genius and even scored a late goal. It was a match Johan would always remember – even if he was the only one smiling in the dressing room!

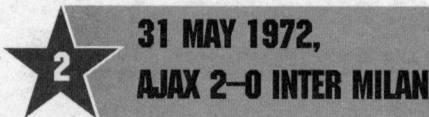

2
31 MAY 1972,
AJAX 2–0 INTER MILAN

Johan loved the European nights, and he saved his best for the final in 1972. In a tight game against Inter Milan, he led Ajax to their second straight European Cup, scoring two goals in the second half as Total Football hit new heights. This final was played in the Netherlands, and Johan got the party started for the thousands of Ajax fans in the stadium!

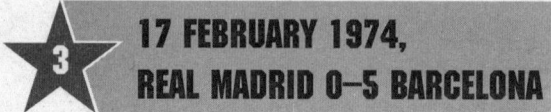

3
17 FEBRUARY 1974,
REAL MADRID 0–5 BARCELONA

The Barcelona-Real Madrid rivalry was legendary, and Johan couldn't wait to experience it. On this day, he silenced the Bernabéu with his mazy dribbling, just adding to his hero status with his new club. He scored one goal and set up another as Barcelona delivered a five-star display and took another step towards the Spanish league title. *Vamos!*

4 19 JUNE 1974, NETHERLANDS 0–0 SWEDEN

This game featured one of Johan's most lasting legacies – the Cruyff Turn. With all eyes on the 1974 World Cup, he left a Sweden defender in a daze with his fancy footwork. See ya! It was a moment of magic that summed up Johan as a true entertainer, and soon everyone was trying it.

5 26 FEBRUARY 1984, FEYENOORD 4–1 AJAX

After his second rocky exit from Ajax for Feyenoord, Johan was fired up to face his old team. Bring it on! Ajax had won the first battle of the season, but Feyenoord were ready for the rematch. Though Johan felt many different emotions in this battle, it felt great to score with a thumping strike into the bottom corner. A few months later, Feyenoord were league champions!

TEST YOUR KNOWLEDGE

QUESTIONS

1. What was the name of the Ajax groundsman who gave little Johan his first job?

2. Where did Johan and his friends play their street matches?

3. Which Ajax manager gave Johan his first team debut?

4. Where did Johan meet Danny, who would later become his wife?

5. True or False: Johan and Ajax won their first European Cup against AC Milan in 1969.

6. In which year did Johan win the Ballon d'Or for the first time?

7. Who did the Netherlands lose to in the 1974 World Cup final?

8. Name the two US clubs that Johan played for in the NASL?

9. When Johan left Ajax for the second time, which Dutch rival club did he join?

10. True or False: As Barcelona manager, Johan won four Spanish league titles in a row.

PLAY LIKE YOUR HEROES

CREATE MAGIC ON THE WING
LIKE JOHAN CRUYFF

STEP 1: As a dribbling wizard, your team is counting on you to create a match-winning chance. Get into space, call for the ball and don't be afraid to try something unexpected.

STEP 2: You're out on the left wing when you control the pass. Take a quick look around you. If the defender tries to mark you tightly, THIS IS YOUR CHANCE! Turn inside and fake a cross.

STEP 3: Now it's time for the Cruyff Turn magic! Instead of swinging in a cross, drag the ball back behind you with the inside of your boot. GENIUS!

STEP 4: But don't just stand and admire your skill! While the defender is still off-balance, get to the ball and dribble down the wing. You're a step ahead now.

STEP 5: After all that hard work, make the most of this opportunity. Take your time and pick out a teammate in the box. GOOOAAAALLLL!